BRIGHTON & HOVE CITY LIBRARIES

Hove Library
182–186 Church Road, Hove BN3 2EG

Tel: (01273) 290700
www.citylibraries.info
for online renewals

To renew please have ready:

- Your library card number
- Your PIN for online renewals

Return or renew by the due date to avoid fines

02560827

RIVER OF DREAMS

Gabrielle O'Hara, a bush pilot in Brazil, plans to enlist the aid of her childhood friend, Nicolao Hamilton, to help her return a conquistador's gold sunburst medallion to a shrine deep within the rain forest. Unfortunately, Nic thinks the trip would be suicide, so Gabby has no alternative but to shanghai him. But things go terribly wrong after they replace the medallion, and as they face relentless danger together, Gabby and Nic's friendship grows into a love that will bind them forever — if they can survive.

SHARON K. GARNER

◆

RIVER OF DREAMS

Complete and Unabridged

First published in the
United States of America

First Linford Edition
published 2002

This novel is a work of fiction. Names,
characters, places, and incidents are either
the product of the author's imagination,
or, if real, used fictitiously.

British Library CIP Data

Garner, Sharon K.
    River of dreams.—Large print ed.—
Linford romance library
    1. Love stories
    2. Large type books
    I. Title
    823.9'14 [F]

    ISBN 0–7089–9786–4

Published by
F. A. Thorpe (Publishing)
Anstey, Leicestershire

Set by Words & Graphics Ltd.
Anstey, Leicestershire
Printed and bound in Great Britain by
T. J. International Ltd., Padstow, Cornwall

This book is printed on acid-free paper

To my sister Pat, and my nieces,
Kim, Tammy, and Brandy. And to
the memory of my mother,
Alma Marie Plowman.
It started with all those late
shows we watched together.

1

'If that plane won't fly, *amigo*, you'd better be able to walk on water.' Nic Hamilton leveled a rifle at her, clicking off the safety to punctuate his cold words.

At the first sound of his voice, Gabrielle O'Hara looked up from where she knelt on his splintered dock, examining her pontoon plane's damaged float. This was a fine start, she thought, Nic playing with guns and threatening her.

'Try *amiga*,' she answered, laughter in her voice. She slowly tugged off her aviator sunglasses, revealing emerald-green eyes, peeled back the baseball cap that confined her coppery hair, and stood up. 'Hello, Nic.' Her voice surprised her when it caught on the edges of his name.

'Gabby.' His face went slack with

shock, erasing the anger. She watched his fighting stance relax and he lowered the rifle, clicking on the safety. His dark eyebrows, thin and sweeping, briefly lifted into his forehead before he squinted at her in the bright sunlight.

'I should have guessed it was you, Gabby. I've heard that you're a madwoman in a plane,' he finally said.

Nic's shouted threats had stopped pouring from her radio before she landed. She'd been a captive audience, since her plane's radio wouldn't transmit, just receive.

She shrugged. 'There's always method to my madness, Nic. I'm sorry I couldn't answer you on the radio. I wanted to surprise you anyway.'

'You wanted to surprise me,' he repeated tonelessly and, at last, smiled his crooked grin. 'Even when I'm threatening to blow you out of the sky if you try to land? But then you never listened to me when we were kids, Copper Top. Why should it be any different now?'

2

She returned his grin with a shaky one of her own. 'Come on, Nic. I kind of guessed you didn't really have an anti-aircraft gun trained on me. And you would have broken me like a twig if I hadn't listened to you when we were kids.'

Hearing both her nicknames on his lips had caused her breath to catch in her throat. Nic and her father were the only people she had ever allowed to shorten her name to Gabby, and Nic was the only one who dared to call her Copper Top.

She pushed the memories back where they belonged, willing herself to get on with her plan. She'd have to be firm with Nic to secure his help in returning the medallion to the shrine, especially if it meant involving him against his will.

She swallowed hard then gestured toward the red and white plane sitting alongside his damaged dock. 'I'm sorry about your dock, too. I had a slight problem.'

Her single-engine plane, which she had just landed badly, was slow, overloaded, and difficult to maneuver.

He started to walk toward her. 'I noticed. You landed that thing like a ruptured duck. The dock can be fixed but what about the plane? I hope you weren't ferrying it for someone.'

She smiled at his analogy and slid her sunglasses on so she could watch him saunter onto the long dock, and to hide what she was thinking. Nic had always been too good at reading her eyes.

She studied him for several heart-beats. Gone was the insecure sixteen-year-old kid she remembered. He looked taller and his slimness had matured into corded muscle. There wasn't even an echo of awkwardness in the man he'd become. Now, he had a boneless kind of grace.

'No, it's mine,' she said when he stood in front of her. 'It's funny you should mention a ruptured duck. This was dad's 'second best' plane and he called her The Ruptured Duck. We tore out the six passenger seats to expand the cargo area. She's old and slow and I don't use her much. My big amphib is being overhauled in Sao Paulo.'

The small lie nagged at her. This is for his own good, as well as mine, she reminded herself silently.

She had a rule about her planes: nobody touched them except her. If she crashed, it would be because of her own stupidity, not someone else's. She had left her treasured old amphibian safely in Sao Paulo because, as much as it hurt, The Duck wasn't coming back. It was overloaded with fuel and supplies. Enough fuel to get them upriver but not back again. Enough supplies for the time it would take them to paddle out on the river.

Together they knelt to examine the slash in the top of one of the plane's floats. The plane was riding low in the water and the float had slid under the dock when she taxied up to it.

'Do you still have the acetylene torch, if I need it?' she asked.

'Yeah, it's here somewhere.' He cocked his head to one side and looked at her. 'Where you headed?'

She concentrated on the damage, deliberately making her voice casual as she rose to her feet. 'Upriver. Want to come along?'

He studied her for one long, excruciating moment before he answered. She almost squirmed before looking away.

'No, I don't. There's nothing upriver but the mission hospital at Grilo and a hundred ways to die. Besides, there's trouble between the Nunes and the Amaral Indians up there.'

She studied the river while he spoke, her body hot and sticky. The Brazilian rain forest sucked the breath right out of her. Then she was uncomfortable and uneasy. The Rio Sonhos, River of Dreams, was running higher than she expected, its dark water already creeping into the thick jungle vegetation along the banks.

Her voice had an edge to it when she finally spoke again. 'Well, you're the district officer for that area. Do something about it.'

He grunted. 'In name only. Besides, my predecessor was a heavy-handed bastard. I'll bet the Nunes and Amaral have long memories.'

She touched the camouflaged, clay-covered gold medallion, the reason for this journey, hanging around her neck beneath her khaki shirt.

'Being the district officer in name only, you won't stop me from flying upriver?' she asked carefully, watching him.

Standing in his shadow, literally, she saw that he carried a new measure of width in his adult shoulders, making him slim at the hips and light on his feet. At six feet three, Nic, the man, had a powerful presence.

His gray-blue eyes glinted. 'I won't have to. I have pop rivets, metal sheeting, and an acetylene torch, but no fuel for ducks, ruptured or otherwise.' He gestured toward a hangar a few hundred feet off the river on a pond-like backwater. 'I have enough in my plane to reach the nearest boat that can get me to Manaus. That's it.'

She jutted out her chin. 'Did I ask for fuel? I brought extra. The Duck will fly without your pop rivets, metal sheeting, or torch, and gravity always gets me down, one way or another. Want to check my cargo, Nic?' she added softly, insolently.

He frowned, drawing his startling eyes to slits in his tanned face, a skin tone compliments of his Brazilian mother. His American father, her father's best friend until the medallion, had given him his height and eye color.

'Maybe,' he said, all friendliness gone from his voice and face. 'And I won't ask first. There was a lot of air traffic over here six months ago. They wouldn't talk to me either. What's upriver, Gabby?'

She'd gone too far, too fast. Her attitude had pushed her into a corner she couldn't afford to be in. Now, how to get out of it?

Her childhood experiences with Nic had taught her that she could sometimes distract him by creating a diversion, changing the subject, or making him angry.

She shrugged and punched him playfully on the arm. 'Lots of trees. So, how have you been?' she said in a rush. 'I heard you went to the States for a while, went to school, got married.'

She'd heard other things, too, like he was divorced and drank too much and was almost a recluse up here since he returned two years ago.

'And I heard no man has ever gotten you to the altar,' he shot back.

She grinned. 'It isn't for lack of being asked.'

'Poor devils.' Nic had learned to play the game. He abruptly changed the subject back to tricky ground. 'I also was informed, by headquarters no less, that you're flying for Manoel Prospero. He does business just one step inside the line.'

That wiped the smile off her face,

and she knew she looked guilty. She was just congratulating herself on leaving her sunglasses in place when Nic reached out and pulled them down to the tip of her nose.

She couldn't tell him just yet that Prospero had owned the medallion and once held a huge IOU from her father. Or explain that it was necessary for her to do business with him to pay off the debt and buy back the medallion. Or that it turned out to be a big mistake to trust his people. Not yet, even though she realized that all he saw in her eyes was guilt over one illegal cargo she'd been tricked into carrying. With one finger she shot the sunglasses back into place.

'I don't fly for him anymore,' she said tersely. 'Do you have a shower that works?'

He studied her a long, frowning moment before he answered. 'Sure. Most of the gadgets still work around the place. I have solar power now. No more generators or kerosene lamps, except in the rainy season.'

Up close she could see and smell more subtle differences in him. His lower face was shadowed by several days' worth of beard. Above it his eyes looked like the maps of interchanges around two gray-blue lakes. His cut-off shorts were filthy, as was his tee shirt which shouted the merits of a seedy bar in Manaus. He looked dangerous.

'Really?' She made a point of looking at him from his uncombed hair to his boots before she pushed her sunglasses up into her hair, deciding to take her chances. 'I flew a load of goats once that smelled better than you. Is this your new look?' she asked sweetly.

'Uninvited guests have to take me as I am. Not staying long, I hope?' This was accompanied by another cockeyed grin.

She ignored him and dug inside the plane for her bag. 'Lead on, Nic. I have to go to the bathroom.'

As she walked the familiar half mile to the house, she fell silent at his side.

She remembered the first time she experienced the suffocating sensation caused by the climate. It was the same day she fell in love with the mighty rain forest.

She had been eight years old and newly motherless. Her father, a botanist, decided to follow his lifelong dream, plant collecting in the Brazilian rain forest. He contacted his old friend Wynn Hamilton, an American geologist and prospector living in Brazil, who had a motherless nine-year-old son, Nicolao. Because they had no close relatives, her father brought her here with him, the first of yearly visits with Nic and his dad for the next seven years.

That first time, she had ridden in an old open-top Land Rover on this same narrow, black earth road she now walked. She had sat in the back with the strange, dark-haired boy who asked her to call him Nic.

Closed in by vegetation, the road was a steamy tunnel, the heat and humidity wrapping around her in a warm, wet blanket. Beyond the road, magnificent trees rose two hundred feet to a leafy canopy.

She had caught splashes of brilliant color in the low, lush growth along the sides of the road. Having inherited her mother's love of flowers and her drawing ability, she wanted to reach out and push aside the tangle and examine the tantalizing blossoms more clearly.

Nic, sitting across from her on the bench seats in the back, had watched her. 'It's shady and fairly open in the forest itself, but don't go outside the compound without one of us. You can get lost in a minute if you go into the jungle.'

She'd followed that advice until that last plant hunting season, the time the men went upriver without her and Nic, farther than ever before. That's when their fathers found the tiny shrine in the jungle and the solid gold sunburst medallion inside it that changed their lives. Not for the better.

Nic broke into her reverie by putting

out a hand to bring her to a halt. His touch brought an immediate feeling of warm tingling awareness of him. When she looked down at her arm in surprise, he snatched his hand away as if her skin burned him.

'Look, you're welcome to stay for a few days if — if you want to,' he said harshly, the cost of the words evident on his face. 'But don't expect me to be good company. I'm off people, especially women.'

'I heard. I'm sorry,' she replied softly.

He looked at her for a moment in silence. His voice, when it came, was that of an unsure sixteen-year-old again. 'How about you. Are you okay?'

She smiled at him fondly, swallowing the lump in her throat. 'I'm fine, Nic, thanks. This will be just like old times.'

His features tightened and he shook his head, suddenly angry. 'What the hell are you doing flying for Manoel Prospero, Gabby?'

She came right back at him. 'I don't fly for him anymore. Look, can we discuss this later? I'm tired, I'm hungry, I'm dirty, I — '

' — have to go to the bathroom. I know,' he said and stalked ahead.

She ran to catch up. She could see the house now, or what was left standing of it. A dun-colored wall had enclosed it and the outbuildings in the old days, rearing out of the jungle to form a courtyard. That wall marked the boundary beyond which she had been forbidden to pass alone. She vividly remembered the day that last season when she had overstepped that boundary.

It had been a strange season to begin with. At sixteen, Nic was edgy and given to long silences and even longer stares. He was the same old Nic, but there had been something else making him restless, something that she had been too immature to understand.

She was her father's sketch artist for the plants he collected, and she had been eager to practice that morning in anticipation of his homecoming. So, while Nic was busy elsewhere, she took her drawing pad and pencils and went outside the wall, into the rain forest, leaving the safety of the road behind. She marked her path on the trees with a bright oil crayon she took for that purpose.

Time and her fingers flew quickly as she tried to draw everything she saw. After a few hours, she had no trouble finding her way back to the road. As she walked toward the house, she heard the Land Rover roaring up behind her. Playfully, she turned around and stuck out her thumb.

Her smile died when she saw the fury on Nic's face. A muscle worked relentlessly in his tanned cheek and his mouth was set in a grim line. He erupted from the driver's side of the vehicle and crossed the distance between them in two strides. His long fingers bit deeply into the soft flesh of her upper arms.

'Where have you been?' he exploded.

'Sketching in the forest. And I blazed

a trail. Now take your hands off me.' Anger and astonishment were mixed equally in her voice.

Her words fed his anger. 'You know you're not supposed to leave the compound alone,' he ground out between clenched teeth. She squealed in alarm when he scooped her up in his arms and dumped her in the passenger seat.

She shot to her feet, leaning over the windshield. Her words followed him as he strode around the Land Rover and got in. 'I don't know what your problem is, Nic, but I'd rather walk than ride with you right now.'

'Shut up and sit down!' He grabbed the tail of her khaki shirt and jerked her down into her seat as the Land Rover leaped forward.

'You're a pig, Nic!' She slapped him on the arm then rode in heated silence, her arms crossed tightly across her chest as she held angry tears at bay.

When they reached the inner court-yard, outside the *sala*, the drawing room, they got out as one and marched inside. Everything of importance was discussed in the *sala*.

She turned to him, hands on hips. 'Now just what was that about? I'm not an idiot, you know. I have jungle experience, the same as you.'

He paced back and forth in front of her in agitated silence, something in his eyes jerking on the leash. She had made him angry in the past, but this time he seemed ready to explode. For one scary moment she wished that he was in a cage, with bars separating them.

'This compound is an island in the jungle — civilization stops at that gate,' he finally managed, barely calm enough to say the words clearly. 'There are plants, animals, and insects out there that are capable of killing you, and you know it, besides the danger of getting lost. And I'm responsible for you when our dads are gone.'

'Since when?' she said and poured on the disbelief.

'Since day one,' he bit out. 'The same

day I told you never to go outside the walls alone.'

'Well, it's different now. I've been coming here for seven years. I can handle myself in the jungle because you taught me how. And I don't want to hear any more about my being your responsibility.' She started for the door.

Nic stepped in front of her, blocking her path. She forgot that he could move like lightning. For just a moment she let his eyes swallow her, reveling in the strange sensation of falling into their gray-blue depths.

'I thought you were lost in the rain forest. What could I do by myself to find you?' he said, a catch in his voice.

She sorted out fear mixed with blazing anger and realized how much the admission had cost him. 'Oh. I didn't think of that. I'm really sorry I was so thoughtless, Nic,' she said contritely. 'Next time I'll leave a note.'

'Next time?' he spluttered. 'There will be no next time, Gabby! *Comprehende*?'

She realized then how white-hot angry he was. Nic peppered his English with Portuguese only when he was under strong emotion.

But she was in no mood to back down. 'I said next time, Nic,' she repeated slowly. 'I'll talk to Dad when he gets back about where I can and can't go. Touch me again and they'll be calling you Lefty,' she warned as he took a step toward her.

He stopped and she stood her ground, rubbing her upper arms where she would carry the marks of his fingers for a week.

His beautiful eyes narrowed to glittering slits as they stared into her green ones across two feet of space. In the sudden stillness she could smell the soft musky scent from his damp shirt.

Her gaze dropped to his mouth where her eyes bumped across the chiseled points of his upper lip then slid along the fullness of his lower. In the next instant she was crushed against that damp shirt and those unbelievably soft, unexpectedly warm lips were on hers.

For a moment she froze in surprise then trembled as her hands pushed their way into his thick hair to hold him while she kissed him back. He finally broke the kiss, staring at her, wide-eyed.

'*Deus!*' The word came out of his mouth in a croak.

In the next second she was so angry she couldn't see him clearly. How dare he bring *that* into it? It wasn't fair! She punched him in the stomach and ran out of the room. The next day their fathers returned with the medallion.

She had figured out a lot about what was fair between men and women in the twelve years that had passed since then. But she had never since been kissed by a man without remembering that first kiss from Nicolao Hamilton.

Reliving it now, she tripped over her own feet. She cleared her throat and kept her eyes on the road, hoping he would let it pass. Out of the corner of her eye she saw his sideways glance and his slow grin and braced herself.

'You're still poetry in motion, Gabby.'

'Oh, shut up, Nic,' she muttered and stomped ahead.

2

Gabby seldom slept in the daytime, but following a quick shower, she slid between the cool cotton sheets of her old bed and fell asleep almost immediately. She awoke as the light coming through the screened, louvered windows and door was fading in the sudden tropical nightfall.

She lay still for a while listening to the chorus of grunts, trills, and croaks coming from the surrounding forest. It was good to be back. And she was stunned at how much it meant to her to see Nic again.

Crashing thunder and a sudden downpour made her stir uneasily. Her timing for this trip was way off, but she couldn't face Prospero or leave Brazil until the medallion was safely back where it belonged. It was already raining steadily in the mountains. She and Nic would have to set out immediately, before the rains got heavier up and down the river.

A gentle knock sounded on the door. 'Gabby? Are you awake?' Nic's voice called softly.

She pulled the sheet higher. 'I'm awake.'

'May I come in? I brought you some coffee.'

'Coffee,' she said to herself, coveting the steaming cup she imagined in his hands. 'Give me a second, Nic.'

Her bag held the basics and they didn't include a robe. She hurriedly dug out some fresh underwear and a clean shirt, pulling on both and buttoning up as she made her way across the room.

A blast of cool air smelling of rain and rotting vegetation struck her with force when she opened the door. It plastered the shirt against her body. One tail in the front flipped up in the gust, exposing a roundly curved hip and white cotton panties. Quickly pushing it down, she stepped back and held the door open for him to enter.

His eyes skimmed over her, lingering on the length of leg showing below her oversized khaki shirt.

She saw the look and saw him swallow before he stepped inside. Working closely with men, she had learned to simply ignore or downplay any notice they took of her as a woman.

'Coffee,' he said in a strained voice, shoving the mug at her. 'You were a coffee head when you were fifteen. I assumed . . . '

'I haven't changed.' She accepted the mug eagerly, closing her eyes and taking a sip before she spoke again. 'Thanks, Nic. Have a seat,' she said, indicating the rattan chair beside the bed.

'No,' he said loudly, taking a step backward toward the open door. 'No, I just came to tell you we can eat in about an hour. You go ahead with — whatever. I'll be in the *sala*.'

The door slammed behind him. She

stared at it a moment, shrugged, then turned away.

This time she filled the deep, footed tub. With a cry of disbelief and delight, she noticed on the shelf above the tub the bubble bath she'd brought with her that last season. She poured some under the running tap. It was weak, but it smelled of roses and made bubbles.

Nic was right, most things still worked around the place, and it was relatively clean. She had been surprised to find that with clean sheets, even her old room was as ready as it could be for her unexpected return.

As she lay there, she grinned at the realization that she was in the middle of a jungle. She was still smiling when she dried herself on one of the thick soft blue towels.

She used the same towel to dry her hair after she washed it at the sink. There wouldn't be time tomorrow and heaven knew when she would be thoroughly clean from head-to-toe again. They would head upriver as soon as she repaired the float in the morning.

She dressed and stepped outside. All the rooms in the long, low house opened off the verandah, with the gate into the walled garden in the middle. She'd check out that old haunt later. She made her way to the double screened doors of the *sala* at the far end and went inside.

From behind the bar Nic leisurely surveyed her loose, wet hair, oversized khaki shorts and shirt, tan and white socks, and sturdy, root-brown boots. She shivered slightly in the warm night when he raised his glass to her in a silent salute.

He, too, wore clean tan khakis, and he had bathed and shaved. Seeing him standing there in the soft light, she realized he'd be alone only by choice in Sao Paulo or Rio. Nic had grown into a ruggedly handsome man.

He pushed his long hair off his forehead and her frisson of self-consciousness departed, to be replaced by a wave of affection for the boy who had become this troubled man.

'You need a haircut. Again,' she said into the silence and felt a slow smile begin.

It was a long-standing joke between them. Gabby had spent a lot of time each season trimming Nic's mane of thick hair. Most of the time she kept her own chin-length auburn waves and curls pulled up in a high ponytail and secured with a ruffled elastic band. She'd left it loose tonight so it would dry more easily.

'Are you volunteering?' He grinned at their joint memory.

'As always. After dinner.'

He indicated his drink and raised his eyebrows in a question.

'No, thanks,' she answered.

'How about some sherry? I have some here somewhere.'

While a medley of bottles pinged against one another from beneath the bar where Nick had disappeared, a tiny, wizened Brazilian with skin like tanned leather shuffled in and placed a plate of cold melon on the small table set for two.

'Luiz? Luiz is that really you?' She ran to him and was enfolded in the old man's arms.

Luiz had been their inadequate but lovable chaperone, nurse, cook, and housekeeper when their fathers left them at the compound. When she and Nic were older, the men had taken Luiz along with them, and sometimes all of them trekked into the rain forest.

Luiz had been old then. She guessed he must be eighty now. Here was a possible ally, especially if she had to give Nic the sleeping pills she'd brought as a last resort to get him aboard the plane.

When Nic reappeared, waving a bottle, she shook her head and quickly looked away, afraid that her thoughts would be written in her eyes for him to read. She hoped this act of faith would rectify what was horribly wrong in their lives.

She watched the old man shuffle

away. 'Luiz still takes care of you? I was afraid I was going to have to cook.'

'I was afraid you were going to offer.' Nic came around the bar to stand in front of her.

'I've gotten better at it,' she said in her own defense. 'Can you believe they went off and left us alone like that? We could have gotten into the kind of trouble they apparently never even considered.'

His eyes glinted in the light as he stood looking down at her. 'I remember that thought crossing my mind a few times. Let's eat,' he added hurriedly, as she felt shock race through her.

Melon was followed by Portuguese beans, thick with some kind of canned meat, heavily seasoned, accompanied with fresh bread, crusty and still warm. Thick, black coffee followed.

'Haircut or chess game?' Nic inquired.

'Haircut, then you can clearly see your defeat,' she answered.

'We'll see.' He called to Luiz to bring

a comb and scissors and two old towels while he carried a bar stool into the middle of the room.

She didn't have clippers, so she layered his hair in the back as best she could. Cutting hair was something else she was good at because of all the practice Nic had given her. She cut her own hair, too.

'Tell me about your dad, Nic. How did he die?' she asked gently as she snipped away.

He sighed. 'I don't know. He's still out there somewhere. I'm sure that's how he would have wanted it to end. Maybe he went too far upriver again and couldn't get back.

'I know our lives went down the toilet after they took the medallion,' he continued. 'Losing your dad's friendship was the first blow. He started to drink heavily after that.'

The conversation was heading in the right direction, she thought to herself. 'I'm sorry, Nic. I agree with you about the medallion. Our lives changed, like yours. My dad believed that by taking the medallion, all of us were cursed and that nothing would change unless it was returned to the shrine.'

He sighed heavily. 'Well, we're forever cursed then. We don't know where to find the medallion or the shrine.'

She jumped, making a cat step in Nic's hair, when she felt the medallion slide across her skin with her movements.

'What happened to you and your dad after that last season?' he asked in turn.

She was cutting the top front, standing in the space between his knees. Nic watched her face. She caught his clean, soapy, man scent, so she stepped back, pretending to check her progress.

'I'm sure you've heard some of it through the Brazilian grapevine. That's how I've kept up with you through the years.

'We went to Sao Paulo, after the medallion was sold. Dad added our savings to that money and bought an amphibian and then The Duck later. After I finished school and got my pilot's license, I flew with him. We worked for an air service and he went plant hunting in his spare time. It wasn't often. Three years ago a plane he was ferrying to Brasilia crashed in a storm. He was killed. I think he died the way he wanted to, like your dad.'

She hesitated before rushing through the worst news. 'He gambled, Nic, and I didn't know until Manoel Prospero arrived with a huge IOU and an empty slot on his pilots' roster. It took what was left of dad's insurance money and seven months of flying for Prospero to pay off the debt.'

Nic leaned back suddenly. 'So that's why you flew for him.' He relaxed and touched her arm briefly. 'I'm sorry, Gabby. Like I said, cursed forever.'

'What if we had the medallion, Nic? Do you think it would make a difference if we returned it?' She waited tensely.

He shrugged. 'Who knows. Maybe, if

superstition counts for anything.'

'But would you want to try? If we could find it and get it back, I mean.' She circled around him, combing and snipping stray hairs, preventing him from seeing her face.

'Not on a bet. It would be a suicide trip. Our fathers were lucky they got back at all. I don't have a plane that will fly that far upriver and back again.'

She looked up to see him watching her in the mirror above the bar with dawning suspicion in his disturbing eyes.

'You're finished,' she said, looking away quickly and hiding her disappointment.

She allowed herself another moment of guilt over her plans for him. If she handled it a moment at a time, maybe it would get easier.

She leapfrogged to a new subject when he turned on the stool to look at her. 'Are you as good at chess as you used to be?'

He frowned, his eyes sparkling and his voice taking on an edge. 'I'm better than I used to be.'

'Is that a challenge?' She carefully removed the towel from around his neck and folded it inside the towel full of hair under the bar stool.

He went out to the verandah, took off his shirt, and shook it out. 'More of an experiment,' he said, coming back into the room as he buttoned it up. 'I play against myself or with a friend on the radio because Luiz still won't learn the game. I've been playing white into a trap.'

'And I'm white?'

'You're white.'

She crossed the room to sit on the couch. A game was in progress on the chess table in front of it. She studied the board while Luiz served more dark, rich coffee. Finally, her hand shot out and moved one of the white chess pieces. Nic's eyes bored into hers and he muttered something devastating in Portuguese.

She laughed. 'I'd like to see you try it.'

She leaned back against the musty cushions. While he pulled up a worn wine-red satin armchair and pondered his move, she looked around the long, graceful, yet utilitarian room.

One wall was lined from floor to ceiling with shelves of moldy books. The couch she was sitting on and several winged-back armchairs were the only furniture. Three inlaid wooden tables that shared an ancient, threadbare Oriental rug in front of a small fireplace had belonged to Nic's Brazilian mother. Across the room was the dining area. An office with a short-wave radio had been tucked into a corner.

'I love this room, Nic. The house is still beautiful inside,' she ventured.

'I could cheerfully put a match to it sometimes,' he said, his gaze flicking around the room before returning to concentrate on the chessboard.

She found herself studying his face

and its expression of fierce concentration. When he made his move, it brought her bolt upright. Now, it was her turn to be studied while she considered her answering move.

Nic remained an aggressive, dangerous player. Although she used all her wits, honed skills, and strategy to escape his trap, he won the game in the end.

'I demand a rematch.'

'You'll get one.' He held out his hand to her and she nestled hers against his palm. He shook it lightly then held on, his thumb moving across the back of her hand in maddening little strokes. 'You're always a worthy opponent, Gabby.'

His long fingers enclosing hers felt warm and safe, just as his presence had been her security all those years ago.

'So are you,' she said quietly, squeezing his hand then withdrawing hers. 'Thanks for letting me stay, Nic. I think I'll go to bed now. I want to fix the plane tomorrow morning.'

He unfolded himself from his chair. 'I'll walk with you.'

They discussed what she might need for the repairs and where she would find the items in the outbuildings. At the double screened doors leading onto the verandah, he reached around her to turn off the lights.

She felt his hands settle on her shoulders as he gently turned her around to face him. For one breathless moment she thought he was going to kiss her. She wouldn't have minded at all, she admitted to herself.

Instead, he asked softly, 'When are you going to tell me the reason you're going upriver?'

She corralled her thoughts as they galloped off in different directions. 'Tomorrow, I promise. I hope you'll agree to come with me.'

Nic's voice was clear and cutting. 'Don't count on it. One thing, Gabby, off the record. Is your cargo legal?'

'I don't fly contraband, Nic,' she answered with as much dignity as she could pack into the words, though she could name Manoel Prospero on her resume. 'The cargo is me — and supplies.'

He acknowledged this information with a curt nod. 'Then does this sudden desire to visit your old buddy Nic have anything to do with the sunburst medallion?'

He was quick. She shrugged to cover her confusion, glad of the darkness. 'What if it does?'

He let go of her, pushed open the doors, and they stepped in tandem onto the verandah. 'That medallion is bad news.' He slammed the doors shut behind them.

She whirled around to face him, her chin jutting toward him. 'And it's why we both lead crazy, useless lives, Nic. We need to do something about it.'

In the reflected silver-blue light from the moon, she could see his eyes flash. 'What the devil are you up to, Gabby?'

She turned on her heel and walked away. 'When you're ready to listen, I'll tell you,' she said over her shoulder.

His voice drifted after her. 'Just remember, I won't let you do anything stupid, Copper Top.'

The silent, peaceful walled garden of her childhood beckoned when she reached the gate in the wall. She glanced back toward the *sala* before lifting the latch. Nic was nowhere in sight but the *sala* lights were on again and the tinkle of glass against glass rode the soft night breeze.

She forced open the rotting wood gate and murmured a little cry at the ruin revealed by the moonlight. There was no beauty or order here anymore. Years of plant debris cushioned the ground underfoot. She knew she shouldn't venture farther but she couldn't help herself. She had to know if their swing was still there.

The path was barely detectable but her feet knew the way. A few seconds later she stood in the little clearing. The woven fiber swing moved in the gentle breeze.

'Here goes nothing,' she muttered and, brushing off the seat, gingerly lowered herself onto it. Nic's handmade Brazilian version of a three-person porch swing had just grudgingly accepted her weight when the beam of a flashlight sent leaf shadows moving all around her.

'Gabby, where are you?' Nic's voice called out.

'I'm here, on the swing,' she answered.

He stomped into the moonlit clearing. 'I thought you were going to bed.'

She couldn't keep the insult out of her words. 'And I thought you were drinking?'

His voice was steel-edged now. 'What are you doing in here? Anything could be hiding in this mess.' He kicked at some leaves with one foot.

A glowing coal of anger fanned itself to life in her chest. 'You're right, it's a jungle in here. How could you, Nic?' she asked, surprised by the venom in her voice.

He flicked off the light. 'How could I what?' His voice cooled off the whole garden.

'How could you let this beautiful place fall down around you like this? You *live* here. What do you *do* all day?' Genuine puzzlement was mixed with the anger in her voice.

'What I do or don't do with my house, what I do all day or all night, for that matter, is none of your damned business,' he bit out.

She took a deep breath to calm herself. It was then she realized that she was swinging back and forth in agitated movement. She slowed the swing's erratic motion.

'You're right, it isn't,' she was able to say in a normal tone. 'I'm sorry. This place has nothing to do with me anymore. But you still matter to me, Nic.'

He moved to stand in front of her so she couldn't swing. 'Go to bed. It's dangerous out here.' District Officer Nicolao Hamilton was evident in his voice.

She crossed her arms over her chest in outright rebellion. 'No, I won't go to bed. Not until you sit down with me on our old swing.'

'It will break,' he explained carefully but impatiently.

She gulped, a lump in her throat crowding the words. 'I know. That's why I want you to sit with me. Better for us to break it than let the rain forest do it. Let's put it out of its misery together, give it the send off it deserves.' She suddenly felt exhilarated, not caring if both of them broke something in the coming fall. 'Sit with me on our swing one last time, Nicolao Hamilton.'

'You're nuts, Gabby. Certifiable. And I have yet to figure out how you talked me into some of the stuff we did,' he protested. Nevertheless, he cautiously lowered himself into his old place beside her, and before she realized it, her hand crept into his.

Together, silently, they swung back and forth just like they had done for hours as children. She was starting to calm down, relax, when the inevitable happened. Without a sound Nic's end of the swing quietly sank to the ground, and Gabby slithered down the incline to land on top of him. He sat perfectly still with her sprawled across his lap, his eyes locked with hers in the silver light.

He smelled of soap and whiskey. In her heart she knew which of them would be his legacy unless he joined her in this act of atonement and returned the medallion.

'There. It's done.' She nimbly jumped to her feet before he could move. '*Now* I'll go to bed. And you, Nic, can go . . . back to whatever it is you do here of an evening.'

3

Luiz was hovering outside her door the next morning when she went in search of breakfast. Nic was still asleep and would be for hours yet, he told her in his raspy, old man's Portuguese. She wanted to talk to him, so she asked him to come with her into the garden.

She could have wept when she saw the remains of the once beautiful place in the daylight. At one time it held a rectangular terrace, pebbled with brilliant, circular patterned mosaic, surrounded by soft green grass and beds of gaudy, riotous plants. Flowering vines had covered the walls and a lattice-work roof had shaded the entire area.

When she and Nic weren't swimming, paddling a dugout, or exploring in the forest, they had spent most of their time here in the garden's shaded beauty, reading, playing cards and board games, talking, fighting, having haircuts, or comparing schools. Nic had boarded at a mission school for part of each year.

The tall wooden gate she'd forced open last night hung on one hinge. Fallen leaves and branches hid the mosaic's beauty while the grass and flower beds were a miniature jungle. The walls had fallen down, along with most of the lattice roof.

Again, she felt anger at Nic rising within her like the Sonhos in flood, even though the state of his home was, as he so clearly pointed out to her the night before, none of her business.

She dragged her eyes away from the decay and turned to Luiz. There was understanding in his eyes when he finished his own survey of the untended garden and looked at her.

'Luiz, I need your advice.' She spoke quietly. 'Do you remember the last plant collecting season my father and I were here? It was the season Senhor

Hamilton and my father brought the sunburst medallion back from upriver. You were with them on the journey.'

Tears suddenly sparkled in the old man's eyes. 'It was the beginning of the end. Sadness and sorrow descended on us all.'

'Tell me what you feel in here, Luiz, when you answer my question,' she said, touching her fist to her chest. 'It's been twelve years. Do you believe it would make a difference in our lives if the medallion was returned to the shrine?'

He nodded so vigorously that his white hair flopped over his forehead. 'It's too late for Senhor Hamilton and your father and me. But it might lift the curse from you and Nicolao.'

She tugged on the rawhide shoelace from which the medallion hung, pulling it up out of her shirt. 'I feel as you do, Luiz. I've found the medallion and I'm going upriver to return it. It's here, under the clay.'

Luiz crossed himself and backed

away from the clay-covered medallion dangling from her fingers.

'I have to work on my plane this morning and I'd like to leave this afternoon. Do you agree that Nic should be with me when I return this to the shrine?'

He nodded, cautiously this time.

'Then I might need your help, Luiz,' she said, touching his shoulder. 'If he refuses, I have something that will make him fall asleep. It won't hurt him. Will you pack what he needs for the journey and help me get him to the plane?'

By the time she finished speaking, his bushy white eyebrows were riding somewhere around his hairline. 'He will be very angry when he wakes up.'

She blinked in surprise then improvised. She would face that Nic when she came to him. 'I know, but it will be too late then. I don't think he'll strangle me if I'm flying the plane.' Her confidant smile slid off her face at his response.

'Perhaps not when you are flying the

plane,' he agreed doubtfully.

Before she hugged him and allowed him to shuffle away, she wrung out of him every nugget of information about that long ago trek and the location of the tiny stone shrine in the rain forest.

After she ate, she returned to her room to change clothes and to hide the medallion before she headed for the outbuildings. In Nic's present mood he might decide to search her bag while she was busy at the dock.

She found what she needed for the repairs just where Nic had told her to look, fearing the whole time she was inside the shed that one or all of the dilapidated structures would fall in on her. An ancient wheelbarrow served as transport for the tools to the river.

Using metal shears, she cut out a sheet metal patch for the tear in the float's thin metal skin. With a cordless drill from the plane, she drilled holes through the patch and the float, cut away the ragged metal, bailed out as much water as she could, then pop riveted the neat repair into place. For good measure, she ran a bead of sealer around the seams. In the end, she decided she'd better check both floats from under-water. She hoped Nic showed up soon to help her.

Just as she finished, he wandered onto the dock. The sun was high. 'Nice job,' he said, admiring her neat patch.

She gathered up the tools and put them into the wheelbarrow. 'Thanks. I didn't need the torch after all. Will you hold a rope for me while I go down to check the floats from below? I hope there are still no piranha or caiman in this stretch of river.'

'I don't think there are, but you'll know soon enough,' he said, uncoiling the rope for her. 'It's running high and fast, so you should be all right.'

She had put on a modest bikini under her clothes before coming to the dock. She quickly stripped off her baggy khaki shirt and shorts and reached for the end of the rope dangling limply from Nic's hand.

He was staring at her, slack jawed, a look she'd seen before on men's faces when they caught her wearing something other than her usual baggy work khakis.

'What's the matter with you?' she snapped. 'You've seen me in a bathing suit hundreds of times.'

He gulped and dragged his eyes, reluctantly she could tell, back to her face. 'Not in that one and not recently,' he croaked.

She kept her voice brisk. 'That's why I wear loose clothing. In my position, I limit my interaction with the other pilots to flying with them. Remember, you thought I was a guy,' she said, knotting the rough rope around her slim waist.

He cleared his throat. 'Yeah, well don't tell anybody. I plead temporary insanity.'

She picked up the loose end of the rope and waggled it under his nose when his appreciative gaze again slid up and down her body. 'Want to take up some slack here, Nic?' She pulled a snorkeling mask over her face and stepped off the dock.

As Nic had said, the river was running high and fast — and red, like sparkling red wine being poured from a giant spout. It reminded her that the Rio Sonhos was one of Brazil's 'black' rivers, which are really red and usually very clear.

Nic had taught her well all those years ago, actually making her commit to memory the information he shared with her about the rivers and rain forest. When she was eight, she learned that the Sonhos takes its color from the rotting vegetation that the rains filter through before running off into the river. It also meant that they weren't bothered as much by mosquitoes here because of the acidity of the water. Nic taught her that 'black' rivers flow south into the Amazon, and that the Sonhos eventually met the big river, although not by way of the Rio Negro, the granddaddy of the 'black' rivers.

Because it was early in the rainy season, the river had some sediment, too, due to the heavy rains in the mountains. She got right up under each float and checked it by touch as well as sight to make sure both were sound. She caught glimpses of Nic watching anxiously each time she came to the surface.

Finally, she swam to the side of the long dock. 'They both look okay.'

She used handfuls of water to clear her clinging hair from her face then Nic helped her out. When she stood dripping on the dock, her fingers fumbled with her tether. The slipknot had tightened in the saturated rope and refused to loosen. The prickly rope was chafing her skin and she wanted it off.

'Here, let me see if I can get it,' Nic said, stepping up to her.

She gasped when his warm fingers slid beneath the rope against the cool, wet skin of her stomach. Nic froze, looking down at her. She went quite still herself, looking back through her clumped lashes while water from the Sonhos dripped off the end of her nose.

'I'll — just — cut it,' he said finally, digging in his shorts pocket.

She expected his old pocket knife. Her eyes opened wide when he came up with a small but efficient-looking switch-blade, which zinged to life with one tiny movement of his thumb.

'Umm, Nic, I don't need anything removed except the rope,' she said urgently, her eyes following the flashing blade.

His voice was gentle. 'I'll keep it in mind, Copper Top.' He tugged on the rope to get some clearance between it and her bare skin. Instead, the action jerked her even closer to him. Again, a stillness came over her as she looked up at him.

'Sorry,' he muttered. To her amazement, his cheeks actually flushed.

She gave him an impatient look then pulled back slightly and held the rope away from her skin with both her thumbs. The razor-sharp knife sliced through the hemp. As soon as she was free, she turned away and pulled on her shirt and shorts. She heard him click the blade back into hiding.

'Luiz sent me to tell you that your lunch and my breakfast are ready,' he said in a strained voice. When she turned back to him, he was coiling the rope into the wheelbarrow.

'I'm starved. Do you think he'll pack some sandwiches for me? I want to leave after I eat,' she said as they started toward the house.

Nic pushed the wheelbarrow ahead of him. 'So soon? I thought you were staying a few days.'

She avoided looking at him. 'I want to beat the really heavy rains.'

Distrust instantly colored his words. 'We have a couple of weeks yet before they hit here. How far will you be going and how long will you be gone?' He stopped and dropped the wheelbarrow handles.

She kept walking. 'I'm not sure.'

He caught up with her and swung her around to face him. There were white lines around his mouth and a muscle pulsed in his jaw. 'Whatever you're into, Gabby, it is not my problem,' he said coldly. 'You weren't here. Haven't seen you, haven't talked to you for twelve years.'

Her quiet voice was laced with sarcasm. 'Thank you for your trust, Nic.' She looked down pointedly at his fingers wrapped around her upper arms.

He let go of her. He dragged his next words, protesting, into the daylight. 'Why don't you stop on your way back? It's been good seeing you again.'

Against her will she looked up at him. 'Same here,' she answered, aghast when her voice wavered.

His eyes locked with hers, then he started to swear, softly and fluently in two languages.

'Well,' she said when he stopped. 'That was a thoroughly disgusting demonstration of gutter Portuguese.

And, boy, am I impressed,' she added, grinning.

'Yeah, and you better hope I am,' he spat out.

He took one step closer to her and she couldn't have looked away if a creature from *Jurassic Park* had peeked over his shoulder at her.

He continued in a deceptively quiet voice that made her want to back up. 'Because after you shower and change, I want to know why you're going upriver, Gabby. If you lie to me, and you know I'll know if you do, I will tear that plane apart.' He paused, and she never realized until that moment how much fire the human eye could convey. 'And then I will strip search you.'

Her eyes grew round and her jaw dropped in astonishment. It took ten seconds for her to find her voice. 'F-Fair enough, Nic.'

* * *

'Okay, let's hear it,' he said ten minutes after they silently dug into reheated Portuguese beans. 'And cut to the chase. Why are you going upriver?'

'I thought you understood last night.' She took the medallion from around her neck and laid it on the table between them. 'To return this to the shrine.'

He picked it up, threw it down, jumped up, and started pacing. 'I don't believe it. You're risking your life. This is insane! Why?'

She turned in her chair to stare at him, stubbornly mute for a full minute. 'You know that, too, if you'll only admit it. And don't you dare laugh.'

He stopped in front of her, towering over her, with his hands on his hips. 'Believe me, there's nothing to laugh about. Enlighten me.'

She gestured, first at him then at herself. 'Look at us, Nic,' she began haltingly. 'You sit up here drinking, neglecting yourself and your responsibilities, while I blow around the country like a leaf in the wind, trying to be one of the boys and hiding the fact that I'm a woman. A few months ago I caught myself spitting and scratching myself. And I was alone. If we give this back, maybe we can lead normal lives.' She turned her head to look down at the medallion on the table. 'Don't you want to be happy and normal?' she asked wistfully.

He started pacing again. 'I tried that, Gabby. I earned a degree in geology. Had a wife and a — divorce. And here I am.' He paused briefly to look at her then he pulled himself up sharply and his voice hardened. 'Being what you call normal isn't all it's cracked up to be.' He started his restless movement again.

She had seen pain flit through his eyes before he turned away. 'I'm sorry, Nic. But I'd still like to try it for myself. All of it. I want to find a nice man, get married, and have some babies.'

His voice was punishing. 'And you think that piece of gold is stopping you? You bought into your dad's theory about the medallion's cursed big time.'

She jumped up and started pacing, too, in the opposite direction. 'After all that's happened to us since they took it, after all you've been through personally, don't tell me you can't feel it, Nic. There's something off balance, out of kilter, in our lives. Happiness slips by an inch out of reach. I never felt this way until after the medallion.'

The words poured out of her in a flood that she couldn't have stopped and didn't try. 'Even though my life was strange by all standards after my mother died, I loved it and I was happy, especially when I was here with you. Something happened to all of us after that last season. I can't explain it, and I certainly don't understand it, but I can try to do something about it. I want a normal life, Nic,' she shouted into his ear as they passed each other.

He threw himself into his chair. 'Good luck. Where did you find this thing? Are you sure it's the same one?'

'I'm sure.' She stopped beside the

table and looked down at him holding it in his fingers. 'My dad took pictures of it before they sold it, and I compared the carvings on it, a bird, a monkey, a jaguar, and sunrays. I found it . . . in a private collection in Sao Paulo and bought it. I asked a friend to put the clay on it for camouflage.'

'How can you possibly return this, Gabby?' he reasoned, his anger spent. 'Our fathers went so far upriver that last time that they had to leave the plane and trek in so they would have enough fuel to fly home. All we know is that the shrine was near the Nunes village.'

'We know enough for now, Nic, and the Nunes can tell us the rest.' She placed her hands flat on the tabletop and leaned toward him. 'My cargo, which you're so worried about, is just extra fuel, camping supplies, and food. Enough for two. I plan to fly the whole way to the Nunes village and use an inflatable raft to come downriver.'

He fell back in the chair and gaped at

her. 'And ditch the plane? It will take you weeks to get back.' He sat up. 'Do you know how many sets of rapids there are up the Sonhos?'

'It's in flood. We'll scoot right over them,' she shot back.

'Twenty!' he screeched. 'And several waterfalls.'

She swept away those problems with the flap of one hand. 'We'll portage around them and the worst of the rapids.'

He closed his eyes and muttered something in Portuguese that sounded like a prayer. 'And what about the Nunes and the Amaral fighting over hunting territory?'

Her voice took on a pleading note. 'I can't help you negotiate a settlement with the Indians, Nic, and I know the trip won't be easy, but the medallion is your burden, too. You should be a part of this. Say you'll come with me. Please?'

He jumped up and started pacing again, no set pattern this time. To keep from getting stepped on, she sat down in his chair and waited.

He ran his hands distractedly through his hair. 'This trip promises everything, Gabby. Besides a wild river in flood, you offer a possible plane crash, unfriendly Indians, heat, rain, bugs, and heaven knows what else. Much as I'd like to share this suicidal adventure with you, I'll pass. And you will, too,' he ended quietly.

She jumped to her feet, fearing what she knew all along was coming. 'What do you mean?'

'I mean I'm not letting you do this.' He sounded weary and she realized the words gave him no pleasure. 'As the government district officer for this area, I forbid you to fly upriver. I'll radio it in to make it official. You'll go to jail if you disobey my orders.'

Her voice was scarcely audible even to herself. 'Don't, Nic. Please. This means a lot to me.' She jammed her hands into her pockets and turned away from him.

'I'm sorry, Gabby, but somebody has to stop you. This is suicide.'

Her trembling fingers encountered the tiny bottle with three sleeping pills in it. She'd forgotten them for a moment. She'd been told that two would act quickly and that three would not harm him but simply induce a deeper, longer sleep. It had to be now, she decided, or she would lose her courage.

She heard him walk away from her to the other side of the room. With her body shielding her actions from him, she poured their coffee and tried to tap two pills into his cup. All three plopped in. So be it. Sliding the empty bottle into her right breast pocket, she thoroughly stirred the dark liquid and turned around. He was looking at a map of the Sonhos that hung on the wall above the fireplace.

'Your headquarters will be surprised to hear from you. Do you think they even remember you're up here?' she said raggedly as she walked over and handed him his cup, unable to meet his eyes.

'They know. I'm not as negligent as you think, Gabby.'

Her head came up at the pain in his voice, just in time to see him take a sip. She almost stopped him. 'Won't you reconsider, Nic? Please?' she begged, the words tumbling over each other in her haste to get them out.

He frowned and shook his head. 'It's for your own good, Gabby. Find some other way. Give the medallion to a church or something.'

Turning away, she saw Luiz watching from the screened doorway. She gave him a tiny nod as Nic drank down more of his coffee. He set his empty cup on the mantel.

It took a half hour for the pills to work. She used the time anxiously restating her reasons for the trip. He listened with waning attention, but he remained adamant. Finally, brushing her words aside, he took a few determined steps toward the radio in the office corner then came back and stopped in front of her.

'An' 'nother thing,' he started to say, pointing one finger in her direction. His eyes crossed as he tried to focus on her.

Gabby's hand crept to cover her mouth as she was overcome by guilt and fear. 'Oh, Nic, I'm so sorry.'

'Gabrielle O'Hara,' he said clearly and horribly, taking a shaky step toward her. 'What have you done?'

She backed away toward the couch and he followed, step by unsteady step. 'S-Sit down, Nic.'

A strangled noise escaped him as he stood swaying in front of her. His eyes, when they focused on her, blazed with anger. 'You're under arrest,' he managed before they closed.

Relieved this part was over, Gabby tapped him lightly in the middle of his chest. He toppled, like a felled tree, onto the cushions.

She gulped. 'It's for your own good, Nic. And mine,' she explained to him softly. She did not sound convinced.

4

She and Luiz got Nic to the plane with some difficulty and strapped him in. He alternately snored or breathed deeply through the afternoon and night, curled up in a fetal position in the co-pilot's seat. And it was a blessing. At least she knew he was alive, because he never moved to prove the point.

She landed near a sandbar in late afternoon, in time to go to the bathroom, eat a snack, and refuel as much as the plane would hold, before night fell. Leaving Nic where he was, she spent a restless night stretched out in the back, between the fuel drums strapped to the sides of the cargo area. She took off when dawn streaked the sky. Nic started to moan.

Sometime later, he said quietly but distinctly, 'I will kill you, Gabby.'

She jumped at the sound of his voice.

'I'm sorry, Nic.'

He was quiet for a while, and she waited in suspense for his next pronouncement. When none came, she glanced at him, just to make sure he was still breathing.

He impaled her with a glare from one reddened eye, the other still being closed and squashed against the seat. 'You shanghaied me on this suicide mission.'

'I know,' she said miserably. 'I'm really sorry, Nic,' she repeated.

'You're going to jail, Gabrielle O'Hara.' He recited in a hoarse voice a list of charges he could bring against her for sins committed against a government district officer.

'For being one in name only, you sure invoke the position's power often enough,' she muttered. 'And you'll have to make up your mind.' She adopted a bantering tone. 'Remember, I can't go to jail if you kill me.' His eyes were closed again when she looked at him to gauge his reaction.

Twenty minutes later he said, 'I haven't decided yet. You won't know which it will be until I strangle you or slap on the cuffs.'

Her forehead wrinkled in a frown. 'I doubt if Luiz packed your handcuffs.' Brightening, she asked, 'Do you really have handcuffs, Nic? Cool.'

'Luiz, too. He always liked you better,' he stated in detached surrender. '*Et tu* — whatever.'

She jumped to her elder friend's defense. 'He's still loyal to you, Nic. He just agrees with me that our lives will be better if we return the medallion. He packed your stuff and helped me get you to the plane, that's all.'

His voice rose above a whisper for the first time. 'Why can't you understand? There's a good chance we won't survive this trip to live out our better lives. How *did* you get me to the plane?' he added, a spark of genuine interest in his voice.

She was happy to share her and Luiz's trials with the formerly limp, dead weight they had to transport over the long road to the river. 'That was tough,' she began. 'Do you remember that rackety old wheelbarrow I used to — '

He interrupted her, saying something very rude in Portuguese. His voice was getting stronger all the time, she noted.

'And just what did you and your geriatric partner in crime give me?' he asked with deadly quiet that, by its contrast to his voice a moment ago, caused her to glance at him uneasily.

'Sleeping pills? At least that's what I asked for.' She hurried on when he growled deep in his throat. 'M-Maybe they were a little strong. And Luiz didn't help me with them at all. He had nothing to do with this. Really. I-I take full responsibility.'

'Pills off some street corner in Sao Paulo, I suppose.' The words had trouble getting through his clenched teeth.

'No, from this sort of doctor I know,' she said in a tiny voice. 'In Sao Paulo. I'm really, really sorry, Nic.'

'Even my hair hurts, Gabby!' It was an accusation.

'I think we should land now. For a little while.' She gave him a nervous sideways glance. 'You'll feel better after you've had a little exercise, some coffee, something to eat, and a few aspirin. Besides, I need to stretch my legs.'

He groaned when she started their descent. 'That decides it. I'm going to strangle you, Gabby,' he said, lifting a limp hand in her direction.

'No you won't, Nic,' she said quickly. 'See how much it hurts when I do this?' She banked the plane in a steep, diving turn into the wind.

He yowled and grabbed his head. 'Don't do that. I'm going to die,' he added matter-of-factly.

'Stop whining. We're almost down. You'll feel better in a little while, I promise.' I hope, she added silently.

The floats touched the river in a smooth landing, and she managed to avoid all the biggest pieces of flotsam shooting downstream. She taxied to the sandbar she'd spotted from the air.

'We can get out now,' she informed him brightly.

In one jerky motion he sat up, twisted around, and opened the door. Then he threw up all over the nice white sand.

Making sympathetic noises, she unfastened his seat belt and helped him out. The dark coffee Luiz put in the big thermos was still hot. She poured him a full measure and carried it to where he sat on the sand, offering two aspirin on the palm of her hand. Before she poured herself a cup, she watched him closely examine the tablets then take them with some of the strong brew.

When they finished, she handed him his bag. 'I'm going to find a tree. You can discover what goodies Luiz packed for you and clean yourself up a little.'

She knew he had everything he needed because she had gone through the bag and also gathered up any equipment she thought he might require, including his machete, rifle, and ammunition.

He dropped the bag. 'I can't make a fist,' he said in amazement, trying unsuccessfully to flex his fingers.

That's how she left him. Using his machete, which badly needed sharpening, she gingerly cut a ragged swath through the thick growth along the river's edge. A hushed exclamation of delight escaped her when she broke through into the forest proper.

'It's like a cathedral! I'll never get used to it,' she whispered to herself.

Green-yellow light filtered through the stained glass window of the treetops and lit the pillars of the huge tree trunks that held up the canopy roof. The forest floor, relatively clear of undergrowth in this area, was carpeted with a thick layer of fallen leaves.

She kicked at them, remembering how Nic had explained the ecosystem to her when she was new to the rain forest.

'You think the soil is rich because

everything grows so good. Right?' he had asked her.

He continued importantly at her nod, appointing his nine-year-old self to educate her in the wonders of his jungle world.

'That's what everybody thinks. But the topsoil is only a few inches deep in the rain forest. The nutrients are in the dead leaves and stuff on the surface. They're recycled into the plants through fungus and mold. That's why the 'slash and burn' method of clearing land is so bad for the forest.'

She was vaguely aware that Nic had trailed along behind her on a wobbly course into the same rain forest that delighted her still.

'Then take those things off so you can see it,' he growled in response to her soft words of a moment ago.

She flinched when he pulled off her sunglasses, folded them, and tried to shove them into her left shirt pocket. He succeeded on the third try. His fingers lingered a moment and he blinked when they found the firm swell of her breast beneath the material. He jerked his hand back.

'Besides,' he went on, 'I need to see what you're thinking. Have to watch my back.' He stared at her owlishly, not quite focused.

'I'm thinking I have to go to the bathroom.' She scanned the trees surrounding them.

He gestured broadly and she ducked just in time. 'Pick a tree, that's what we're here for.'

He walked away and without hesitation she followed him, looking around her with pleasure. Her training from ages eight through fifteen kicked in automatically. When they were in the rain forest together, Nic took the lead and she never let him out of her sight — except for one thing.

He stopped suddenly and she ran into him, knocking him over. 'This is my tree,' he said, sprawled against the huge trunk where her momentum had brought him to rest. 'Want to share?'

'What? Oh. I, umm, forgot.' Her face burning, she backed away then turned and walked in the opposite direction.

They regrouped on the sandbar where they shared the sandwiches and fruit Luiz had packed. After that she left Nic to his own devices and took shelter under one of the plane's wings to sleep, telling him to wake her in three hours.

In two, his indignant howls woke her. Just in time, too, since the river had risen and was lapping at the edge of the blanket on which she lay.

'What's the matter?' she asked, jumping up and pulling the blanket after her.

Nic, bare chested, was digging in his zippered bag like a terrier. 'That malevolent dwarf didn't pack any clothes except my khaki uniforms!' he thundered.

'So, blow your cover, D.O. Hamilton. At least they're clean. You were going to let me get soaking wet,' she finished in an injured tone.

Mistake. She realized it the moment

she saw the look in his eyes and the expression on his shaven face. Nic was back. Full strength.

He threw down the shirt he was holding and slowly walked toward her. 'You're damn right I was. It would save me the trouble of throwing you into the river, just to see what's biting today. There's a lot of payback coming for what you did to me, lady,' he said in a voice that made the hairs on her neck stand on end. Never had she heard the tones of anger honed to such a polished, cutting edge.

With every step he took toward her, she retreated a step, barely noticing the curly dark hair that covered his chest and stomach and disappeared into his khaki shorts.

'N-Now, Nic, don't do anything I'll have to hit you for,' she said edgily as he drew ever closer.

'Just try it. In fact, do it. Please. I'll call it resisting arrest and act accordingly.' His eyes burned into her with white-hot anger as he ground to a halt in front of her.

She let out an involuntary squeak when he took her by the shoulders and gently squeezed them together until she felt like a turtle peeking out of the collar of her oversized shirt.

'I'd like to know something, Gabby. Tell me what you thought would happen when I came to.' He delivered the words in a conversational tone that sent chills up and down her spine.

Boy, was Luiz right, she thought to herself. Nic was very angry when he woke up.

She swallowed hard. 'I c-concentrated on trying to make you understand why you should be here with me. I didn't let m-myself think about how you would react, Nic.'

'Well, it's time to think about it,' he shouted into her face. 'I'm bigger than you and I'm stronger than you, Gabby. What's to stop me from throwing you into that plane then taking the controls?'

Early in her life she had learned that

tears were useless and a waste of time. She allowed herself very few. She was surprised now to feel one of the pesky things slide uninvited down her face.

She gulped and thrust out her chin. 'Not a thing, Nic. *This* trip,' she said softly but with steely determination in her voice and eyes.

The pressure on her shoulders eased until his hands merely rested there. She saw his eyes widen as he followed the progress of the tiny drop down the curve of her cheek. With one thumb he gently brushed it off her skin.

'I could throttle you with one hand and you stand there telling me to go to hell with those eyes,' he whispered. 'This really means that much to you? You'd come back and try it alone?' he asked, bewilderment in his voice and shock in his eyes.

She nodded slowly, never taking her gaze from his.

He looked upriver at the high water and thick rain forest before he heaved a sigh and let her go. 'I must be friggin' nuts, as crazy as you,' he mumbled. 'Come on. I'll help you refuel The Duck, Copper Top.'

'Thanks, Nic,' she whispered and turned away.

'Just a minute,' he said and every inch of his shirtless self was Authority. He held out a hand to her, palm up. 'I'm confiscating the rest of those pills.'

She reached into her right breast pocket and handed him the empty vial. 'I only had three and I . . . ' her voice trailed away at his look.

'Gave them all to me at one time? You could have killed me!' He stomped off to where his bag lay.

'No, he said three would be okay. I guessed your height and weight.' She followed him, pleading her case, leaving out that she had grossly underestimated both. 'Nic, you're the closest thing to family I have. I didn't want to hurt you. Pills were the only way I could think of to get you on the plane if you wouldn't agree to come with me. I'm truly sorry for what I did to you.'

He was shrugging on a short-sleeved uniform shirt, with bright patches on the shoulders, and stopped momentarily at her words. 'Not nearly enough to suit me. I still owe you, Gabby. Big time.'

She sighed, hoping he would calm down soon. She couldn't stand it when Nic was mad at her. This trip would last forever if he didn't forgive her.

He went off like a rocket again when he climbed into the cargo area and saw the number of 50-gallon drums of aviation fuel she had strapped to the sides of the plane.

'I told you I was carrying extra fuel,' she peevishly responded to his outburst. 'There are so many because I couldn't handle the 100-gallon drums.'

He gaped at her. 'I should be grateful you just took out a piece of my dock. If you had crashed you'd have taken out the whole house!'

'It's falling down anyway,' she spat, then calmly reminded him to pump from a drum on one side of the plane and then from one on the other, alternating, so the load would stay balanced. 'She's handling better already,' she added.

'Oh, well, that makes me happy. Like riding an armed bomb,' she heard him mutter as they set about their task.

'I'm using your radio to call in,' Nic said when they were finished.

She cleared her throat. 'Oh, umm, I lost the radio right before I got to your place.'

He stepped closer to her, holding her eyes with his. 'You didn't happen to disable it, did you, Gabby? So I couldn't call in?'

She allowed what she thought of that question to show in her eyes. 'I don't play games with the safety of my plane or my passengers, Nic.' When his glance darted to the fuel drums and back, she flushed. 'We can receive but we can't send. That's why I didn't answer you when you were shouting such colorful abuse into your radio at the house before I landed.'

She involuntarily stepped back when he raised his fists and his eyes to heaven, beseeching a higher power to please just look at what he had to put up with. Then he went forward into the cockpit.

He took the controls and Gabby wouldn't have argued about it if her life depended on it, because she wasn't sure yet that it didn't. This was a new Nic beside her.

'*Deus*, Gabby. This thing is flapping its wings to take off!'

'She's old, slow, and overloaded, Nic. Be gentle with her.'

She hid behind her sunglasses and slept or watched the endless rain forest slip by below. Occasional rapids broke the surface of the Sonhos and small tributaries, some nameless, joined its flow. As thick and green as dyed puffs of cotton, the giant trees of the forest grew almost to the water's edge. The total effect, as far as her eyes could see, was like a dark rope twisted in the folds of a green blanket.

They passed over one small Indian village then the mission station at Grilo hove into view. Nic banked the plane into the wind for a landing.

She put her hand on his arm. 'No, Nic, you agreed to help me,' she said urgently.

'Somebody needs to know where the hell we are, Gabby. I can use Dr. Aguerro's radio and just maybe he'll have what we need to fix yours,' he reasoned.

'But the river's rising,' she wailed. 'And we're wasting time and fuel!'

He summed up his feelings on those scores in one colorful word, then he settled the plane lightly on the surface of the water.

He sent her a measured look. 'That's something you haven't explained, you know. Why now? Why so desperate to return the medallion now instead of waiting for the dry season?'

A tall, slender man had stepped onto the dock in anticipation of helping them tie down the plane. She used him as an excuse to avoid Nic's questions.

'Later. Who's that?' She sounded like an out-of-sorts child and she didn't care.

She wanted to slap the look of tolerant amusement off his face. 'Dr. Paul Aguerro, a friend of mine.'

Dr. Aguerro turned out to be in his early fifties. With white at his temples and big brown eyes, he was handsome, and gallant with it. He hugged Nic and pounded him on the back when they greeted each other. He bowed over Gabby's hand and kissed it when Nic introduced her.

'So, you are Nic's Gabby,' he said, studying her closely while still holding onto her hand. 'But I will call you Gabrielle and you must call me Paul. Nic speaks of you so often I feel I know you.'

Startled by this information, Gabby glanced at Nic and was surprised to see him scowling at Paul Aguerro's hand which still enclosed hers. With a self-satisfied smile that she didn't understand, Paul released her when he saw Nic's look.

'He needs civilizing, this one,' he said to her as he swept a hand in invitation in the direction of a sturdy barracks-style house perched in a clearing. 'You should visit him more often,' he added with a smile.

Close by was a much larger building, which she assumed was the hospital. A small Indian village had sprung up around it. Lined up for introductions in front of the hospital were three nuns in white nursing habits. Paul did the honors, then invited Nic and Gabby into the house for something cool to drink and a light meal.

The nuns followed. They said little but were friendly and efficient. They served iced coffee and potted ham sandwiches then disappeared.

'We have few patients right now, so they and I get three times the attention,' Paul observed, watching them leave.

'Now,' he said briskly. 'You are

welcome anytime, my friend, but what brings you so far upriver?' he asked Nic.

Nic's eyes met Gabby's and she stubbornly held his gaze until he looked away to the doctor. 'Gabby has convinced me to try to sort out the trouble between the Amaral and the Nunes.'

Paul gave a low whistle. 'But the season! And your small plane! Surely you will have to take to your feet to have enough fuel for your return flight?' Concern was written plainly on his even-featured face.

He turned to Gabby. 'It's a journey fraught with danger. Will you stay here as our guest while this madman continues upriver?'

Gabby gave him her sincerest smile. 'I thank you for your concern. Actually, I initiated this trip. Nic and I have something else to do upriver, something we have to do together.'

Paul looked from her to Nic and back again but refrained from asking. Nic turned the conversation to the radios, and Gabby excused herself to freshen up. When she got back Nic was using the mission's set. Paul had no spare parts for the plane's radio.

'Let me show you my hospital.' He held the screened door open for her, maintaining a steady flow of conversation. As soon as they were outside, however, he stopped and lowered his voice.

'I'm worried about Nicolao, Gabrielle. It's not good for him to be so isolated. He still mourns his little son.'

She sucked in her breath, dizzy for one second as she absorbed the impact. 'Wh-What? Nic has — had — a son?'

As her lips formed the next, obvious question, he held up one hand to stop her. 'He shared his sorrow in confidence. He must tell you about it himself. I thought you knew or I would not have mentioned it.'

She shook her head to clear it. 'I-I believed this trip upriver would change both our lives for the better, but I had

88

no idea Nic had experienced something so terrible.'

'He has told me a little of your journey, but not all, I think. It is a worthy one, though ambitious and dangerous. I will ask my sisters of mercy to pray for your safety. I've found their prayers to be helpful.' His eyes sparkled beautifully in their brown depths. 'God listens to them, whereas mine often fall on deaf ears.'

She laughed and they walked on. His next words came hesitantly. 'We play chess, Nic and I, by radio. He talks of you often.'

She frowned. 'That surprises me. I haven't seen him for twelve years! Our fathers fell out. We've kept up with each other through gossip on the grapevine.'

'You were an important part of his life, more than you know, I think, and one that has been missing for a long time. Forgive me but ... there are strong feelings between you two?'

She nodded. 'We forged a powerful bond, Nic and I. We were together only four or five months a year, but two lonely, motherless children packed a year's worth of friendship, companionship, respect, and fondness for each other into the time we were together.'

He pinched his lower lip between his thumb and forefinger. 'I speak boldly now. It would be a fine thing for both of you, I think, if your relationship matured beyond the bonds of friendship.'

She laughed uneasily. 'Nic and I?' Then she stopped abruptly, remembering his first kiss all those years ago and how she wouldn't have minded if he'd repeated it the other night.

'Nic and I?' she repeated in a wobbly voice, not nearly as confident now. 'Nah!' she finally said, brushing away the thought. 'We're just getting used to each other as the man and woman we are now instead of the boy and girl we were then. We'll settle into our old relationship soon.'

Paul shrugged good-naturedly and conducted a thorough tour of the well-equipped little hospital. Nic joined them a while later, just as she and Paul were sharing a moment of companionable laughter.

She gave Nic a searching look, surprised that he didn't appear any different to her. Nic, a father. He would be a good one, she decided. His babies would never be lonely or in need of a father's attention.

He frowned at her stare then spoke to Paul. 'I left a note of our destination and a very loose time frame beside the radio. It's all guesswork. There are too many factors involved in this trip, too many things that can go wrong.'

After that, he whisked her to the plane, politely refusing Paul's invitation that they spend the night. Within minutes they were in the air again.

'I like your friend,' she commented when they leveled off.

His voice was flat. 'I noticed. And I noticed he likes you. I hear his leaves from the hospital are one big party. They take him out from the north, the same way he gets his supplies, but he prefers to play in Rio.'

Relieved, she realized it was Paul's reputation that disturbed Nic, not his harmless attentions. 'He probably deserves every minute of it. Play on, doc, I say,' she declared and let it go at that.

They landed on the river at dusk. Shadows were lengthening by the time they secured the plane and slashed an entrance into the forest. The day's heat was dissipating.

'It feels like the forest is waiting for something,' she whispered as they picked a campsite.

'It's waiting for us to make a mistake. Two victims for the price of one,' Nic answered grimly.

When they were ready for a fire, he shaved the ribs of palm fronds until he had a small pile. He set them alight with a lighter and added larger and larger twigs and pieces of wood she gathered until he had a roaring fire going. She opened cans of food and set them on a flat rock in the center. While the food heated, they erected the small nylon tent she'd brought. Its bottom was of the same waterproof material with zippered screening at each end.

'You thought of everything for camping, Gabby, I'll give you that. You can have the tent to yourself unless it rains,' he said, as he put the two sleeping mats and rolled blankets inside then came back to the fire.

She pulled the food out of the flames. They ate thick, smoky, meaty soup with crackers and washed it down with strong, sweet coffee. Gabby rinsed the tin plates, cups, and silverware then dried them on leaves before packing them away until morning.

Thunder rumbled in the distance and Nic cut some palm fronds to protect their supplies from the impending storm.

Gabby lit a small pressure light and carried a basin of water into the tent to clean up. There was more room than she first thought. The light, hissing quietly, lit it well. She tossed aside Nic's mat and blanket and unrolled her own to sit on while she washed. She put on clean cotton panties then buttoned on a clean tan khaki shirt and matching shorts while thunder shook the ground beneath her and lightning lit the tent, making the pressure light seem dim.

The first drops of rain splattered against the nylon when she was fifty brush strokes into her one hundred per night. It was something she remembered her mother doing for her and she practiced it religiously. It kept her thick, naturally curly hair shining and gave her some semblance of control.

'I'm coming in,' Nic announced a split second before doing so.

Gabby froze when, sitting Indian-fashion with the hair-brush in her hand, she suddenly found herself face-to-face with him. He looked at her a long moment before she scuttled backward out of his way, and he turned aside.

Nic unrolled his mat and blanket and laid his rifle across the top of the mat.

'You know better than to bring anything with fragrance to it. The bugs will eat you alive,' he growled.

'I didn't.' She sniffed her forearm. 'It's soap. The smell will be gone by morning.'

He was sitting with his back toward her. Gabby was at the end of a brush stroke when he shrugged off his shirt. The brush went flying out of her hand as the expanse of his satiny, tanned shoulders filled the suddenly small tent.

She retrieved her brush then hurriedly crawled to the flap to empty her bath water outside. She set the basin out in the rain to fill then zipped them in. Shaking out her blanket, she slid beneath it, and he stretched out inches from her.

Outside, the storm broke in earnest in torrents of slashing rain, with all the sound effects accompanying it. Inside the tent, they were snug and dry.

'Ready for lights out?' she asked then gasped when he beat her to it, reaching across the top of her mat to shut off the light.

Velvety blackness engulfed them, so thick that she couldn't tell if her eyes were open or closed.

'What's wrong?' She heard the smile in his voice, which came from above her. Lightning lifted the blackness for a moment, showing her that he was leaning on one elbow on the edge of his mat.

'It's so dark. I forgot how black it is out here,' she answered breathlessly.

'I remember you said the same thing the first time you and your dad came upriver with us. That was the beginning of the best times, Gabby. I hated coming out with my dad before and after that. When you think about it, it's a miracle either of us survived our childhoods,' he said with wonder.

She hoped her quiet tones would softened the gentle reprimand she was about to deliver. 'They did the best they could, Nic, two men with two kids they didn't know what to do with. They kept us with them and they loved us. Surely that's not too bad an epitaph, is it?'

'I guess not,' he conceded. 'Ouch!'

Gabby had attempted to lock her hands behind her head to get comfortable and talk awhile. Nic was still too close and she poked him with her elbow.

'You ought to come with a warning label,' he growled.

'Sorry. Close quarters,' she said, stifling a giggle. She didn't succeed. And she couldn't stop with a giggle.

'Does your nose still wrinkle up when you laugh that hard?' he asked softly, a chuckle lurking in his voice. 'It did when you were growing up. It fascinated me.'

'You tell me. Although there wasn't a lot to laugh about yesterday or today,' she added waspishly.

'You had no trouble laughing with Paul,' he reminded her quickly.

She ignored that. 'Well, you'll just have to wait and see for yourself, won't you?'

'I'll do that,' he said in a husky voice that again came from above her.

She swallowed, wondering what he would say or do next. 'D-Did you ever wonder about the conquistador who built the shrine, Nic?' she babbled, just the slightest nervous quiver in the words.

She was relieved to hear him settle back with a sigh onto his mat. 'No, but I'll bet you have. It's just a theory, you know.'

'There's enough evidence to make it a reasonable theory,' she defended. 'Besides, it just feels right. Remember Dad said they found some fragments of metal near the shrine? He laid them out and they resembled a chestplate and helmet. And museum experts verified the medallion as being of sixteenth-century Spanish origin.'

'The Spaniards came down from the north, didn't they?' There was just a hint of interest in his bored voice. 'See, even they knew better than to come up the Sonhos.'

She didn't acknowledge his dig. 'Yes, but usually not this far into the interior. They came from the north, east, and west, on the rivers, so it's plausible that a lone expedition got this far. I read up on the Spanish explorers. By 1525 they say Spain was inhabited by women because the men were off looking for gold in South America. I've never forgotten one passage that described those men, ' . . . valor and vainglory, murderous cruelty and rock-like endurance.' '

He snorted with disgust. 'All that and they let the Portuguese take Brazil.'

'Just imagine it, Nic,' she said, ignoring his attitude. 'He's the last one left alive out of maybe two hundred men. He knows he can't survive, so he turns to his God. He builds a shrine, puts his most valuable possession inside it, prays, then dies. He created a holy place and we desecrated it,' she ended on a plaintive note.

'We didn't,' he argued.

'Well, by association then,' she

snapped. 'Why don't you believe, Nic? Can't you feel it?'

'No, I can't. Our fathers made bad decisions, Gabby. So did we in some areas of our lives. That's all there is to it.'

'Then why are you here?'

'I'm here because you're here. I still can't believe I'm doing this,' he muttered beside her.

'Well, you are, so can we please just make the best of it? It's like when we were kids.'

He gave a bark of laughter then his voice was rough. 'Not quite. We're not kids anymore, Gabby. You've grown into a beautiful woman.'

'Have I?' she answered in genuine surprise, pleased beyond reason that he thought so. 'I've been told I clean up nicely,' she added, suddenly self-conscious.

He grunted impatiently. 'You must date idiots. Blind idiots. Don't you own a mirror? And tell me again why you dress like somebody's grandmother.'

The warm glow of his compliment was fading fast. 'Does this particular part of our conversation have a point, Nic?'

'The point is that I'm not a kid anymore, either.' He sounded uncomfortable. 'Just keep it in mind, will you? It'll make this trip a lot easier on both of us.'

Shock kept her quiet for a full minute. 'Oh,' she finally said.

'Yeah. Oh. Goodnight, Gabby.' He flounced over on his side, away from her. She knew a flounce when she heard one.

'Goodnight, Nic. And just for the record, I've noticed you're not a kid anymore either. Now that we've been honest with each other and shared our guilty little secrets, let's just forget them, shall we?'

She flounced over on her side, away from him. She knew a flounce when she executed one.

5

An awful roaring and barking tore her from the depths of sound sleep at dawn the next morning. She released her breath in a sigh of relief when she recognized the racket as that of howler monkeys, calling to each other in the canopy. Their pumping roars carried for miles.

She went still when she realized that Nic, still sleeping deeply, was snuggled up against her back. They were nested like spoons, curve to hollow, and she liked it. His chin was in the hair on the top of her head, his right arm rested across her hip, and his long-fingered hand covered most of her stomach.

After an argument with herself, she decided there was no way to gracefully extricate herself without waking him and calling attention to the situation. Besides, he felt so warm and safe against her that she didn't want to end it just yet. When he finally stirred, she closed her eyes and took long, slow, deep breaths, pretending to be asleep. She heard him swear softly, untangle himself, and slide backward away from her.

She waited, eyes closed, listening to the sounds he made as he put on his shirt, socks, and boots then crawled out of the tent. Finally, she sat up and stretched. Before she put on her own socks and boots, she shook them out, the way Nic had taught her.

She packed her knapsack, shook out and rolled up their blankets, then rolled the blankets neatly inside their mats. At last she lifted the screen flap and went out. He was frying fish over a small fire.

'That was quick,' she exclaimed.

'I set out a line last night.' His eyes briefly met hers before they both looked away.

After a visit to a tree and a quick wash in the rainwater that had collected in her basin, she sat down to a plateful of the fish. Nic didn't want to talk and was impatient to get started. She cleaned up the breakfast things and packed them while he took down the tent.

Kneeling in front of the pack that held the cooking equipment, she glanced up at him to ask a question. The glance turned into a measuring look, the question forgotten. Her eyes slid down over his body and she remembered the feel of every inch of it pressed against her back. She turned away while she hid the blush scorching her face.

Carefully, she removed all human evidence of their camp. The empty fuel drums would be the only regrettable indication of their travel through this part of the rain forest. They had no choice but to jettison them. She and Nic, after discussing it, decided that without the weight of the empty drums, they might get a few more miles out of The Duck.

As they loaded and refueled the

plane, she finally remembered what she wanted to ask. 'How soon do you think we'll get to the Nunes village?'

'This morning, maybe, if it's still where it used to be. Paul wasn't sure. Dad said the Nunes have a communal hut. It should be easy to spot from the air.' In response to his worried, preoccupied manner, she decided silence was better than conversation.

She was a little worried and preoccupied herself. This was something she hadn't thought of. The Indians moved their villages periodically to ensure they had fertile soil for their garden plots and fresh hunting areas. What would they do if the Nunes were no longer on the Sonhos, she wondered? Their input was needed to locate the shrine. She knew only what her father had told her and what she had wrung out of the elderly Luiz.

She drew the first shift simply because Nic buckled himself into the co-pilot's seat. They were in the air a couple of hours when Nic sat up straight and asked her to do a high flyover of an area of muddy water that flowed out some distance into the Sonhos' channel. From the air they couldn't see anything in the forest because of the thick canopy of treetops.

'What is it?' she asked.

'I'm not sure,' he answered, curiously intent on what lay below. He scribbled in a tiny notebook he withdrew from his uniform pocket. Whatever he had written, he wasn't going to share it with her.

Sometime later they passed over a large Indian village. 'Amaral,' Nic said. 'They have individual huts. We should have reached the Nunes village before the Amaral village, Gabby. We missed it or they moved.'

She sighed. 'They wouldn't leave the river, would they? What do you want to do? Besides turn around, that is.'

He didn't answer for a minute. 'Keep going. Maybe we'll find the Nunes farther upriver. They'll know more about the shrine than the Amarals.

Besides, if I'm going to negotiate an agreement, I have to visit both villages.'

Hungry, she landed an hour later. Nic took over the controls after their early lunch and by early afternoon the Nunes village finally hove into view, their large communal hut within the clearing unmistakable. A smaller ceremonial hut stood beside it. He landed without incident on the river littered with debris and taxied to the village's river landing.

Gabby saw his quick, casual glance at her turn into a hard calculating stare. 'What?' she asked fearfully.

'Take that band thing out of your hair,' he ordered. 'Put your hair up under your hat then keep it on.'

'Why?' she asked, gaping at him.

He frowned when she didn't move to do as he instructed. 'And once we're with the Indians, do what I tell you, when I tell you. No questions, no sudden moves.'

'You're scaring me half to death,' she answered in a tiny whisper, her eyes refusing to release his.

'Glad to hear it. Maybe there's hope for you yet. Oh, I forgot to tell you,' he added gleefully. 'As far as I know, these Indians still occasionally take heads. I'll bet they don't have a red-haired one.'

She squeaked in alarm and bent forward in the seat, tearing the ruffled band out of her soft auburn curls. She finger combed her hair forward into the crown of her baseball cap and jammed the hat onto her head. When she sat up and looked at Nic, her sunglasses were askew.

He gently pushed them up on her nose with a finger, while one corner of his mouth lifted in a cockeyed grin. 'Keep those on, too, unless I tell you different.'

The armed Indian men gathered in a line along the shore. They were no taller than five feet and had warm brown skin and thick, black hair that was cut in a circle across their foreheads, above their ears, and around the backs of their heads. Red dye streaked their faces, shoulders, and stomachs. A narrow waistband of cotton was the only covering each wore. Small pouches and knives were attached to their waistbands. Some carried blowguns, slim wooden tubes with a mouthpiece at one end, while others held bows taller than themselves. There were no shrunken heads that Gabby could see. They watched them and the plane with suspicion written plainly on their faces.

'We're on,' he said softly and moved to open the door. 'I wish we had gifts for them.'

'I almost forgot! We do.' She ticked off the items on her fingers. 'A machete for the headman, cigars for the men, bead necklaces for the women, string bracelets for the children. In the cargo area.'

He nodded, a half grin on his face. 'Get them but keep everything out of sight for now.'

'Wait for me,' she said and ducked into the back. She searched out the burlap sack of goodies she'd brought for just such an occasion. 'Aren't you taking your rifle?' she asked when she clambered into the cockpit.

'What good would it do? If they want us dead, we're dead,' was his grim answer. 'Let's hope they remember our fathers fondly and that they understand the pidgin I'm about to use on them. It's a kind of soup of all the Indian languages I've ever heard.'

'You always impress me. You're a natural, Nic. I could never get my tongue around any of it.' She meant to simply lay her hand on his right shoulder. Instead, it moved in a light caress across the wide width of both. She jerked it back, since it wouldn't behave.

Nic shouted greetings as they walked carefully on the floats to the shore. They secured the plane under the Indians' watchful eyes. The colorful patches on Nic's uniform were getting a lot of attention. Nic spoke again and Gabby estimated that they exchanged pleasantries for a full five minutes before the Indians reluctantly parted, revealing a path that led through the trees.

'Take me to your leader?' she ventured.

'I guess. How the hell should I know? I haven't spoken this lingo in years. Come on.' He sounded harried!

Gabby hesitated when she noticed women and children in the group, hanging back behind the men. The women's narrow cotton waistbands included a tiny apron of fringe. They had flowers and leaves protruding from their pierced ears and from under the cotton armbands they wore. The women were handsome with their big brown eyes set in high, wide cheekbones. Gabby found herself smiling at them and the bright-eyed children who glanced shyly at her from behind their mothers' legs. At five feet seven, she was a giant among them. The women closest to her leaned forward to look under the bill of her cap and peer at the dark lenses covering her eyes.

Gabby hurried to catch up with Nic who strode up the slightly uphill jungle path without her. The Indians silently fell into step behind her. She was very aware of the blowguns and bows and arrows the men carried.

A quarter of a mile later, they came to a clearing shared by the huge communal hut and the smaller ceremonial hut they had seen from the air. Each had palm-thatched sides and a partial roof. She peeked around Nic's shoulder when he stopped.

A grave-faced, middle-aged Indian waited for them. Iridescent blue feathers were stuck in the Indian's ears and intricately painted red designs covered his chest. Without being told, she knew this was the headman.

Nic spoke in guttural sounds that meant nothing to her. She stayed behind him, but she eased around so she could watch his face from the side. He frowned and he smiled, but mostly he frowned. And she didn't like the pleading tone in his voice at one point.

She jumped when he spoke to her in English without looking at her.

'He remembers my father and yours. Old drinking buddies during their visit, apparently. I also made points by coming unarmed and having a woman with me. Take off your sunglasses and look at the nice man,' he added softly.

She opened her mouth to ask why, then remembered his warning to do as he told her, when he told her, and to do it slowly. She took off her sunglasses and looked at the nice man, throwing in a wide smile for good measure.

The Indian's mouth opened in surprise and he made a little sound. He stepped closer to her and rattled off something to the others who crowded around to look up into her face. She did a slow pirouette, meeting as many Indian eyes as she could. When she again faced the headman, he smiled back at her, warmly, and said something. Nic gasped and blinked before he smiled and nodded.

'W-What's going on, Nic,' she asked,

edging closer to him. 'You look like you've just had a revelation.'

'He says you have jungle eyes, eyes the color of the rain forest,' he said, his voice soft as he stared down at her. 'I've never been able to figure out what it was about your eyes . . . but he saw it.'

He shook his head then continued in a normal voice. 'I was right, they've never seen green eyes before. Now come here and stand in front of me, face him, and take off your hat. I'll bet they've never seen a redhead either,' he said with a sly grin.

Nic was enjoying this too much. She slowly moved to stand in front of him but she didn't turn to face the Indian. 'Does this have to do with payback or — headhunting?' Despite her best efforts, there was a definite quaver in her voice on the last word. She saw a satisfied smile flit across his face and she understood.

'Payback,' he whispered to her, 'plus using the resources I have available to me. He's guaranteed our safety because of our fathers and your eyes. I want to see what I can get in the way of hunting territory for your hair. Do something dramatic,' he added.

'You're still a pig, Nic,' she said, sweetly smiling up at him.

'At your service, Jungle Eyes. Now do it,' he growled.

Once she had watched a shampoo commercial being filmed in a fountain in Rio while she waited for an engine part for The Duck. She envied those beautiful women the chance to make men gasp with their dramatic moves and the smoldering looks in their eyes. For years she'd suppressed her femininity and the sexual side of her nature for the sake of her safety and her livelihood. Here was an opportunity to have a little harmless fun.

'Hold onto your butt, Nic,' she warned and turned to face the Indian.

Slowly, gracefully she folded her body from the waist. With a flourish she tugged off her cap, held it away from her, and dropped it on the ground. She pushed both hands into her hair and shook it out to fullness as she came upright. Then she looked at the Indian through ringlets of hair and half-closed eyes, a model making love to the camera. By chance she stood in a patch of sunlight, creating a halo of burnished copper around her head and face. Silence reigned.

She heard Nic gulp behind her. '*Deus!* You're good,' he finally said in a strangled whisper.

'Felt great. I've always wanted to do that,' she said softly. 'You should have seen it from his point of view.'

'He should have seen it from my point of view,' he informed her raggedly.

She whirled again and a gasp swept through the crowd, from one side of the group to the other and back again. The headman stepped forward and lifted a corkscrew curl off her cheek. He pulled it straight and smiled when it sprang back into place. He said something to Nic who laughed then replied.

'I'm almost afraid to ask,' she whispered shakily.

'You should be, after such a provocative display,' he teased. 'He says he'll take you for a wife if I decide I don't want you. I said I'd keep it in mind.'

She looked up at him over her shoulder. 'They think we're . . . married?'

'Whatever. Do you want me to tell him you're available?' he asked with a grin.

She cleared her throat. 'What would you like for dinner, dear?'

The headman smiled, patted his cheeks, and asked a question, which Nic answered.

'Now what?' she asked nervously.

'He wants to know why your cheeks turn pink. I explained that you're new to the marriage bed and still shy with me. You're turning me into a chronic liar,' he complained.

'Oh, it wouldn't be — ' she said before she could stop herself.

'What — ?' Nic began, but the Indian

117

started to speak.

At the headman's next question, she heard Nic swallow before he fired an answer.

'What? What?' she asked, her nerves stretched to the breaking point.

'Whatever you do, don't slap me, Gabby. Slapping would be bad right now. Got that? Just stand still and — and I'll explain in a minute.'

She felt Nic step up against her back as he spoke matter-of-factly to the Indian. Looking down, she watched his hands slide across her stomach and abdomen in opposite directions, pulling her even more closely against him. One hand cupped her left breast and the other rested just below the waistband of her shorts. The Indians broke into knee-slapping laughter. Nic released her immediately and stepped back.

She stood stock still for a moment then pivoted slowly to send him a withering look. 'Would a fat lip count?'

'Yes, it would.' His voice was taut. 'He wanted to see if you're the same as their women. I told him yes but he'd have to take my word for it. You can strip if you don't like the way I handled it.'

She felt a parade of emotions, shock, indignation, and finally laughter, march across her face as she looked up into his suspiciously bright eyes.

'Time for goodies, I think,' Nic whispered before taking another step back from her. 'The machete first.'

She heard herself give a little gurgle of laughter, then she quickly opened up the burlap sack and dug into it.

An invitation to a celebration that night quickly followed. Their arrival from the sky with former acquaintance status, her green jungle eyes, her hair like a tropical flower, and their wonderful gifts added to the gaiety. Nic was closeted with the headman and elders in a corner of the ceremonial hut until the feast began. As she listened to a storm rock the forest, she wondered what the outcome would be.

She and Nic were the guests of

honor. He winked at her as he took his place beside her on the woven mats in the middle of the floor. The headman sat on Nic's right. The rest of the men sat around them and the women and children were behind the men, closer to the walls. Oily nuts strung on pieces of vine served as smoky candles to light the festivities.

Gabby was looking forward to the meal until they served roasted grubs for starters. She picked one up but could not bring herself to put it into her mouth.

'Eat it,' Nic hissed quietly. 'You'll offend them if you don't.'

Gabby looked away from the fat, white, two-inch long nightmare on her palm and up into Nic's sparkling gray-blue eyes. 'But-But it's a grub!' she managed in a choked whisper.

He shrugged while watching her closely. The gleam in his eyes looked suspiciously like hovering laughter and she figured out it was payback time yet again.

'A roasted grub,' he pointed out. 'Pretend it's one of those crunchy, puffy cheese snacks you used to bring by the bagsful to the house every season and tried to hide from me. It will taste like soft cheese anyway. Close your eyes, chew twice, and swallow. You won't have to eat anymore.'

With her eyes still locked on his, she popped the grub into her mouth, chewed *once*, and swallowed, suppressing a shiver as she did. He was right. The grub didn't taste bad. It was just knowing she had eaten *a grub* that made her stomach lurch.

The smile in Nic's eyes erupted into a startling grin, although his voice held a note of exasperation. 'Stubborn as ever. You always have to do it your way.'

The Indians set before them a feast of roasted wild pig accompanied by thin, yellow plantain soup, manioc bread, and baked yams. After the meal the men smoked their cigars and drank a milky liquid out of tiny, hollowed-out gourds. Gabby sipped hers cautiously at first then took a deep drink of the rich, smooth liquid. The Indian on her left was prepared to top off her gourd from a bigger gourd pitcher.

She noticed that none of the Indian women were given a gourd and were only now eating, after the men had finished. Warmth suddenly shot from the tips of her fingers to the tips of her toes, surprising her.

'What is this?' she asked Nic. 'It's very good.' She held out her gourd to her Indian buddy with the pitcher.

Nic said something to the Indian. The man grunted and stopped pouring when the liquid came only halfway up in the brown half-pint-sized container.

'It's the potent sap of a tree and you should have a healthy respect for it.' He let his gaze wander over her face then linger on her mouth as she licked a mustache off her upper lip.

Under his close scrutiny, she self-consciously pushed a straying curl off her cheek, then forced the hand into her lap when she caught herself doing it. She couldn't help the way she looked. Her hair had taken on a life of its own in the humidity of the rain forest. Before the meal she had again pulled the burnished mass of curls back and up and used her ruffled elastic band to hold it.

She suddenly wondered what Nic's ex looked like. A long-legged, dark-haired beauty was her bet.

She and Nic really needed to discuss this man-woman awareness situation, because it *was* getting in the way. Paul Aguerro had planted the thought in her mind, and she wanted it out of there. Last night's honesty with each other hadn't exorcised it.

'So, how are the negotiations going, District Officer Hamilton?' she asked, pointedly returning his stare then giving him a saucy grin.

He looked away first, a sheepish tone to his voice. 'I forgot how good it feels to do something constructive. We're not there yet, though. That heavy-handed predecessor of mine visited them once at the old location, after our fathers' visit. As a demonstration of his power, he fired a gun. The bullet ricocheted and wounded a child. Lucky for him it was only a flesh wound. But he wore the same uniform as I'm wearing right now.'

She glanced uneasily at the Indians surrounding them. 'Is there anything I can do to help, Nic?'

'I told them that if they won't negotiate with me, the government will send someone else. Better a devil they know, I guess, because we're talking. What I need now is an angle. I have to think of a visible means they can use to divide the area and police themselves, and it has to be fair to both groups. Any ideas?'

Thinking, she stared off into the distance, swirling the liquid around and around in her gourd. The candle flames, wavering in a draft, burned like the sun. They reminded her of the sunburst medallion, and how man had copied the skies in his art since the beginning of time, the stars, the sun, the moon.

'The moon,' she said simply, bringing her gaze back to him.

'The moon,' he repeated with a blank look that quickly turned to one of respect.

She spoke as it came to her. 'The moon is something they can see and understand. Don't divide the disputed territory between the tribes. The two groups can hunt the whole disputed territory according to the wax and wane of the moon. They can always hunt within their own territory.'

He gently took her head between his hands and placed a smacking kiss on her forehead before turning back to the headman.

'Glad I could be of help,' she said to his back, licking the milky liquid off her arm where it had sloshed out of her gourd. She poked the Indian beside her, smiled, and shook the gourd at him. He was getting stingy with the rations.

After the meal, the dancing began. Gabby thought about joining the women in one dance, a simple stomping beat they performed in a circle. She thought better of it when she tried to get up. There seemed to be something wrong with her legs.

She plopped back down onto the mat where Nic was still chattering with the headman, both of them scratching drawings of the phases of the moon into the dirt floor. Waiting a moment, she tapped him on the shoulder.

'Ask him about . . . the shrine, Nic,' she said when he turned around.

Nic put one finger under her chin and raised her head so he could look straight into her eyes. His own eyes narrowed and he frowned. 'Go easy on that stuff, Gabby.' He leaned around her and said something more forcefully to the Indian on the other side of her who had poured the milky substance.

When his eyes met hers again, the chattering, gesturing Indians ceased to exist. The pounding rain, thunder, and lightning outside were silenced. Her breath caught in her throat, and she heard herself gasp softly. Her face grew warm.

Nic didn't have smooth, polished good looks. His were rough, untamed, a little frightening, and fascinating. He had grown into a tawny-faced stranger who made her bow before his temper and blush beneath his gaze.

He liked what he saw, too, because she watched the frown disappear as a gentle smile lifted the corners of his mouth and warmed his eyes. By the time she gathered her wits to return his smile, he had turned back to the headman.

They engaged in a guttural conversation then Nic turned back to her. 'They abandoned the village they lived in during our fathers' time many years ago. It's downstream, beyond the Amaral village. He also says he can tell me how to find the shrine. We have to visit the Amaral village anyway.' With that his attention returned to the Indian.

When he turned away, she picked up her empty gourd and swallowed the last few drops of its soothing contents, hiccuping softly. Return the medallion, get themselves downriver, and then she could leave Brazil to start over. Her only regret would be leaving Nic behind.

Suddenly, her thoughts, her plans, the medallion, and her reason for being there dimmed in her mind. Everything slipped away from her beneath the surface of the milky white liquid she'd consumed. Finding a place to sleep became her new purpose in life.

To make herself heard above the Indians' din, she slid closer to Nic, misjudged the distance, and crashed into him. 'Please, Nic, where can I go to sleep?' Her tongue slipped on the edges of the words.

He gave her a hard look then laughed. 'We've been offered hammocks around the headman's cooking fire in the big hut. Can you walk?'

She drew herself up to her full sitting height and said with dignity, 'Course I can walk. Been doing it since I was a baby.'

After her third attempt to stand, he lifted her to her feet and swung her up in his arms. Her body felt boneless and numb. And just who in this distinguished company was humming 'Spanish Eyes,' she blearily wondered.

The light and voices faded as he carried her out into the now-still night. She snuggled deeper within the hard-muscled support of his arms and pressed her face against the warm skin on the side of his neck. He smelled of rain and wood smoke and . . . Nic. She felt safer and more at peace in that moment than in any since she had said good-bye to him twelve years ago.

Her last sensations before sleep took her were those of being deposited on a gently swaying tree bough that seemed to hug her body, then of being covered with a cloud.

6

Harsh reality returned at dawn. The tree bough turned out to be a woven hammock, and the cloud a cover of mosquito netting. Another hammock, empty, was hanging directly below hers.

Other hammocks and other cooking fires were spaced evenly around the huge circular hut under the protection of the half roof. The sky was visible where the roof ended over the center of the building, creating an open, common courtyard around which the Indian families lived.

Cautiously, she sat up and swung her legs over the edge of the hammock. Other than a slight headache, everything seemed to be functioning reasonably well. Just to be on the safe side, she decided she would sit quietly for a few minutes before proceeding gently into the day.

The circle of cooking fires around the big communal hut was a vision of domestic tranquillity that morning. Young mothers were nursing or playing with their babies. Other women were sweeping the areas around their fires. Still others were weaving baskets, aprons, or hammocks.

One Nunes woman was making manioc bread. Yesterday afternoon, before the feast, Gabby had watched the woman grate the manioc tubers into a wooden trough. The woman had then put the mess into a flexible basket and squeezed out the prussic acid. When she saw that, Gabby remembered her father telling her that manioc was the native form of the cassava root.

Today, the stuff was dry enough to knead into a fine dough. The woman's deft hands spread the dough over a big, flat clay plate over her cooking fire. Five minutes later the thin bread was done.

The peace and quiet was suddenly shattered when Nic appeared, all smile and big voice. 'Good morning, Copper Top. Does your hair hurt?'

It took her a second to focus on him, her first close-up moving object of the day. He was standing over her, busily folding the mosquito netting from the hammock below.

She tried to speak but nothing came out. She swallowed then cleared her throat. 'I'm not sure yet,' she said hoarsely. 'I feel — odd. There ought to be a law against that stuff.'

He stood at his ease, watching her. 'There is, up and down the river, but the Indians still use it in their ceremonies and for special occasions. I did warn you. Twice.'

He leaned over, one hand on his knee, the other pointing at her feet. 'I brought some food earlier and a basin of water for you to wash in. And here's your bag from the plane.'

'Thanks, Nic.' Hungry, she warily reached for a thin, flat round of manioc bread and a banana from the pile of food on a mat at her feet.

'Nic,' she said, horrified, 'I can't make a fist!'

He laughed, a sound that echoed hollowly inside her head. 'This just gets better and better. It's a strange feeling, but it will pass. I've been there, remember, and recently, too. I'll take the controls today so you can . . . whoa!'

He had plopped down on the hammock beside her, flipping both of them onto the mat below and into the middle of the bananas and manioc bread. The Indians didn't even pretend they weren't watching them. She heard laughter all around.

She lay quite still exactly as she had landed, flat on her back. 'Try not to enjoy this so much, Nic. Gloating really doesn't become you.'

He unfolded himself upwards and pulled her to her feet. Surprisingly, her head stayed on. She reversed direction and sat down carefully on her hammock.

'Payback, Gabby, all payback. Don't

get mad, get even, I always say.' He handed her the half-peeled banana, now flat.

'But you did get mad as I remember it.' She felt like stomping her feet and throwing something, a result, no doubt, of her excesses the night before.

'With good reason!' He was suddenly all business. 'Come on, Gabby, let's move it. I checked and we have enough fuel to get to the Amarals and a little beyond that before we have to take to the river. I have to get them to agree to the moon compromise then send a runner back here. They promised not to kill him.'

She swallowed her bad mood with the rest of the banana. 'Not killing the runner is good. Congratulations. You're officially no longer a government district officer in name only. Welcome back to the world of the working stiff,' she said around a mouthful of manioc bread.

He looked thoughtful. 'I guess you're right.'

'I'm proud of you, by the way,' she said, rolling up the rest of the manioc bread and eating it like a tortilla.

He stopped folding her mosquito netting to look at her. 'Thanks for your help. I couldn't have done it without you.'

'You see?' She suddenly felt cheerful. 'We came up here to set things right in our lives and it's working already.'

His reply brought her down to earth fast. 'Don't tempt fate, Gabby. A lot can go wrong between here and home and we can't afford to forget it.'

Humbled, she was reminded that she owed him an apology. 'Nic, I'm sorry about last night. You had enough to think about without me adding to your load. I-I didn't do anything stupid, did I?' she finished weakly, feeling her cheeks grow warm.

Her stomach dropped to her feet when he quickly turned away from her. 'You didn't do anything I couldn't handle,' he said in a strange voice.

'Oh, God, I knew it. That's why I

don't drink much because I have a horror of doing something — I shouldn't. What — What did I do?' she asked in a tiny voice, bracing herself.

'When I was carrying you out of the ceremonial hut — Well, I've never had a woman suck my earlobe before. It was nice. I liked it, you know?' His voice was full of innuendo.

Mortified, she buried her face in her hands and moaned. Then Nic laughed.

She jumped up and waggled a banana at him. 'Age hasn't improved your pig status, Nic,' she spluttered. 'Now you're just a twenty-eight-year-old pig!'

He stepped up to her, his gaze taking a slow journey over her face and coming to rest on one pink cheek. She saw him swallow before he spoke. 'You were fine, unless you count your rendition of 'Spanish Eyes.' You were just . . . snuggly and sleepy, so I carried you across the compound to your hammock. The headman's wife came along to show me where to put you. Okay?'

Somewhat mollified, she looked away and said stiffly, 'Thank you for your help, Nic.'

'Anytime, Copper Top.'

Something in his voice drew her eyes back to his face. He was close enough that she could see tiny, shining beads of water clinging to his dark hair, probably from his morning wash. He was also freshly shaved. She wondered what it would feel like to smooth her fingers along his tanned cheek. She clenched her fists at the thought.

'Oh, thank heavens,' she said, holding them up and clenching them and unclenching them so he could see. 'They work!'

Nic shook his head and grinned. 'Hurry up!' he ordered as he took the mosquito netting and headed for the plane.

They said their good-byes to the Indians at the river landing. With a sinking feeling, Gabby noted that the river level had risen considerably overnight. They were in the air when Gabby asked about the shrine.

'The headman said a rock formation marks the place on the river where we have to land. I think I caught a glimpse of it on the way upriver. The formation continues right into the rain forest and the shrine is built on it not too far from the river. I'm sure it's something Dad would have made a point of checking out. Now that we have a reference point, we can ask the Amarals how far it is downriver from their village.'

She nodded then curled up in the seat and gave herself up to the results of last night's party.

Nic had to wake her when the individual huts of the Amarals came into view in a clearing.

'So, are we doing the Nic and Gabby Road Show with the Amarals?' she asked sleepily.

He gave her a grin. 'You know it. Why mess with a good thing? You don't happen to have any more goodies back there, do you?' he added hopefully.

'I do,' she answered gravely, sitting upright. 'And I expect you to be properly appreciative. We have a machete for the headman, cigars for the men — '

'Okay, I'm grateful,' he interrupted. 'And I'm impressed. It's the long trip home that worries me.'

The whole village, a much smaller number than the Nunes, was waiting for them when they landed on the river. The Amarals were short and handsome with the same shade of bronze skin the Nunes had. Their dark hair was cut short above their ears and eyebrows but the back was worn long. The men had blue-black tattoos spiderwebbing across their cheeks and chests. White bird down was stuck to the bodies of some of them. They were short on smiles, she noticed, and blowguns and bows were once again much in evidence.

It was a wizened old Indian headman who got the green eyes and red hair treatment. She grinned when Nic asked her to wait, then he walked over to stand beside the Indian while she did her hat trick, the shampoo model imitation. The results were the same. Impressed, this headman asked some of the same questions that the Nunes headman had asked, but these were answered without embarrassing results.

He hadn't met their fathers but he had heard about them from the Nunes before each village moved several times and the fighting started. They knew about the former D.O. and the gun, too. Nic would have to use the same arguments here.

At the end of the goodies distribution, Nic frowned, took her hand, and followed the headman who was moving off slowly between the huts, as he admired his new machete. A tiny boy of about three tried to take Nic's other hand but settled for clutching the hem of his shorts when he found his arm wasn't long enough. Nic looked down at him in surprise then smiled.

'Where is he taking us?' she asked, pulling back slightly.

Nic gently jerked her forward, much to the amusement of the Indians following them. 'We're being escorted to our hut. I think.' Nic's voice sounded strange and he wouldn't meet her eyes. She was immediately suspicious, especially when he added, 'They have a special one for us. Apparently.'

The whole entourage came to a halt outside a hut that stood a short distance from the others. The headman spoke to Nic again then left them, followed by the rest of the Indians. The little boy's mother had to peel her offspring off Nic's leg.

Bunches of dried leaves and twigs were tied to the top and sides of the small, low doorway and a larger bunch lay across the doorstep. She crossed her arms over her chest and studied Nic. He appeared stunned.

'Okay, Nic, time to share. What are those? None of the other huts had this stuff. I'm not going in there until you tell me what's going on.'

'I'm not sure. Uh, I think he told me the greenery is supposed to guarantee us lots of babies.' He continued quickly when her eyes grew round. 'It's a wedding hut. This headman wanted to marry you, too, so I told him we just got married. At least I think that's what I told him.'

He looked unsure of himself and glanced after the headman, rubbing his chin as he did so. It sounded like sandpaper. Nic's five o'clock shadow was always early.

Gabby sighed. 'Whatever, as you so cleverly put it when we were with the Nunes. You first, Nic.'

Nic had to get down on all fours to crawl through the low doorway; Gabby managed by crouching. She walked to the middle of the dirt floor and looked up through the opening in the roof to the blue sky directly above. On the floor below the opening a small cooking fire burned. The smoke drifted up the sloped roof and out, a good insect deterrent, she guessed.

'Is there somewhere I can take a bath?' She rubbed the back of her neck with one hand.

'I asked. There's a small pool,' he said absently. 'I'll get your bag from the plane and ask one of the women to take you there.'

When he continued, she was puzzled to hear his voice strain to remain relaxed. His words picked up momentum, telling her he was tense.

'We should stay inside a few minutes, then we can circulate freely. I'll be meeting with the headman and the elders. Don't leave the village unless you go out with the women to bathe or gather food.'

'You're babbling, Nic.' She was more wary than before.

She glanced at the two hammocks in the hut, again one hung directly below the other. When Nic followed the direction of her gaze, she felt her face burn and quickly looked away.

'Don't forget to ask them about the

shrine.' Her voice was sharper than she intended.

He took a few paces around the small area of the hut, looking even more ill at ease. 'Look, Gabby, I don't think we can go out of here looking like nothing happened, especially you.' He stopped in front of her, unbuttoning his shirt. 'You know, swollen lips or something.'

She dragged her eyes away from his slowly appearing, impressive bare chest, then took a step back. 'What are you doing? And don't you dare hit me, Nic.'

He closed his eyes and shook his head before he spoke again. 'I'm not going to hit you, Gabby. When have I ever hit you? I unbuttoned my shirt for their benefit; you just pinch your lips or bite them or something so they get red and swell a little.' His voice was tight on the last words.

She could tell he was holding onto his patience with both hands, but she couldn't figure out why he was upset with her.

She frowned in concentration, looking at him through narrowed eyes. 'I'm slow today, Nic. I'm sorry but I've lost the thread here. What are you talking about?'

He exploded. 'Stop acting like a virgin, Gabby, and a dense one at that. This is a *wedding* hut. I think they sent us in here to — to — cement relations?'

Her mouth fell open in surprise and she immediately covered it with her hands. One out of two wasn't bad, if Nic only knew it. She wasn't dense. Then she started to laugh. The tension between them rode away on the sound.

Nic was grinning when he pulled her hands away. 'Your nose does still wrinkle up, just like when you were a kid.' Then he was suddenly nervous, all business, and in a hurry. 'Listen, I have to go. Come here and I'll show you what I mean. It will only take a second.'

He took her face between his hands and brushed his whisker-roughened cheek across her lips, wiping her smile off as he went.

'Ouch! Nic!' she squealed, prancing and pulling away.

His hands quickly moved down to her arms to hold her still. Before she could gather her wits or put together another word, he rubbed his sandpaper cheek against hers, continuing down the side of her neck in a sweet, burning pain that left her both breathless and speechless.

Then his mouth came down on hers, hard and fast, bruising her lips beneath his own. He pulled back to examine his handiwork, meeting her pop-eyed stare briefly. Then he kissed her again, harder this time. And much, much longer.

Gabby had stopped struggling during the first kiss. Now she couldn't breath, couldn't think, couldn't make her knees do their duty, couldn't remember her own name. She felt only Nic's lips on hers, lighter now and moving gently, and the delicious fingers of fire that scorched her from her head to her toes.

He finally stepped away, letting go of her, and she staggered. 'There, that ought to do it,' he said in a ragged voice, something in his eyes she hadn't seen since that long ago day when he kissed her for the first time.

She blinked, sucked in a breath, and nodded in agreement, bringing a trembling hand to her burning lips. 'It certainly should,' she gasped.

'I'll see you later,' he said shakily and turned to start through the doorway on his hands and knees.

She found her temper, her feet, and the tattered remnants of her senses all in the same moment. 'If I find out you're lying, Nic, I'll murder you! And here's a mark to take with you.' Then she helped him through the doorway with the flat of her boot square on his tight little Brazilian butt.

His howl of outrage from outside gave her great satisfaction. As a precaution, she grabbed a piece of firewood in case he came back inside to 'discuss' her decision. But all remained quiet.

One of the Indian women brought

her bag a few minutes later and she changed into her bikini, hiding the medallion in the bag. She put her shirt on over her suit, picked up her towel, soap, and shampoo and went out.

The young Indian woman was waiting for her. Gabby's pouty lips and reddened cheek and neck were objects of great interest to the woman. There was no one else around to appreciate them. She wished Nic was, so she could kick him again, in the shins or points north this time.

When the woman noticed Gabby's bikini, she made motions for Gabby to remove it. Gabby firmly indicated that she wanted to keep it on. Shrugging good-naturedly, the woman gestured for Gabby to follow her along a path. It led them to a small stream that poured down into a quiet pool before moving on to the Rio Sonhos. There was a wide beach of white sand. Other women and young children were in the water.

After swimming for a while and playing water games with the children, she slipped out of her bikini in a quiet spot and scrubbed herself vigorously before pulling it back on. Then she washed her hair, sharing some of her shampoo with the women, warning them to keep it out of their eyes. A while later, the women and children, answering some silent signal, left in a body. She followed them.

The Indian men and older boys, full of locker-room spirit, were coming down the path as she cautiously picked her way along. Nic, stripped to the waist with a towel draped over his shoulder, brought up the rear. He walked slowly because, again, the little boy ran alongside, holding onto the hem of his khaki shorts. She clutched her unbuttoned shirt together as Nic's eyes skimmed down over her. Her skin tingled as if he'd touched her.

He stopped, blocking her way. 'May I borrow the soap and shampoo? Please.'

Silently handing the bottle and soap holder to him, she willed herself not to blush.

'Still mad?' he asked with a cocky grin.

She smiled back simply because it was Nic grinning. 'I'll forgive your assault since you thought it was necessary at the time.'

'I did think it was necessary, but I hurt you and I'm sorry about that.' He rubbed his backside. 'Your kick is as strong as a mule's, by the way.'

She smiled, all innocence. 'My small contribution to the cause.'

He glanced down at her bare feet and was instantly angry. 'Where are your boots? Do you remember *chigoes*, Gabby? Tiny insects that live around some Indian villages? After they burrow under your toenails, they lay very big egg sacs that have to be dug out. Don't take off your boots again except to sleep or to go in the water.' He edged around her and left her prancing on the path.

She wished she hadn't given him the soap and shampoo after all, because she could have thrown them at him. It would have been impossible to miss because his shoulders were touching the jungle growth on both sides of the narrow path. Since she had no ammunition, she turned and gingerly made her way back to the hut. There she used a packaged, pre-moistened towelette to thoroughly clean her feet and around her toenails before putting on her socks and boots.

They went to the Amarals' long, rectangular ceremonial lodge that night for another feast. Nic's negotiations progressed slowly but steadily, after his threat of another D.O. handling negotiations should he, with no visible weapons and a woman in tow, fail. The runner was to set off at dawn the next morning.

This time Gabby was seated with the women at the back, and the little boy sat beside Nic on the mat. He'd told her that the boy was the headman's grandson. Nic turned around every so often to make eye contact with her and she was grateful to him for it.

This meal started with fruit, followed

by fish then cakes and soup made out of manioc. A fermented drink was served, a potent, cloudy yellow liquid that she tasted out of courtesy then refused, memories of the night before still fresh in her mind. When the men began smoking their stinking cigars, she mouthed a request to Nic that he ask permission for her to go to their hut.

She had brought a small flashlight from the plane and it was tucked into the waistband of her shorts. That and moonlight lit her way across the clearing and down the path to their little hut. She craved some quiet time, and a paperback mystery waited for her in her hammock.

Nic, bless him, had set up the pressure light inside. She lit it and moved it closer to the two woven hammocks hanging in the shadows. He had draped mosquito netting over each, but his sleeping mat and blanket lay on the lower hammock. Nic had sworn he was going to sleep on the dirt floor, since sleeping in hammocks woven by tiny Indians, for tiny Indians, tended to bend his spine in ways God never intended.

She hung her clothes on a twig she stuck into the palm-thatched wall then put on a clean khaki shirt over her fresh cotton underwear. She kept her boots on.

Out of the corner of her eye she caught a movement while she marched around the hut counting strokes as she brushed her hair. She froze when what was moving crawled into the circle of light cast by the pressure lamp.

A tarantula the size of a soup plate was plodding across the dirt floor toward her.

7

Her visitor was covered with reddish hair that appeared to be standing straight up, much like her own at that moment. Although she had come across huge spiders before on her trips into the rain forest with Nic, she could not rid herself of her primal fear of them, especially after seeing a bird-catching spider in action.

Scarcely breathing, except to whimper, she scrambled into the top hammock and pulled all the mosquito netting up off the dirt floor, out of the spider's way. She had her paperback, her flashlight for more direct light, and her hairbrush, everything she needed to keep vigil until Nic came to remove the intruder. She grinned when she recalled that Nic didn't like spiders, either, having been at her side when the pretty little bird flew into that web.

The only good thing about this encounter was that the spider was making a straight line for the only exit. Then it stopped, squatting down on its many legs. And it stayed there, perfectly still, for two hours or more. Her time was equally divided between the murder and the spider. Finally, a scuffling sound from the doorway announced Nic's arrival.

'Honey, I'm home!' He slid through the doorway like he was greased.

'Uh, Nic — ' she began quickly, but he was too fast for her.

He was still in a half crouch when he saw the spider twelve inches in front of his nose. '*Deus!*' he added in a shout as he pushed off into a leap that would have done a pole vaulter justice, landing on the other side of the hut. He even cleared the small fire in the middle.

Gabby erupted into peals of laughter. The more she laughed, the more Nic scowled. He finally sat down on his hammock to watch the spider and to wait for her to stop. The spider didn't pay any attention to either one of them.

'If I could get out, I'd sleep in the plane,' he said plaintively.

'If I could get out, I'd join you,' she said, wiping her eyes.

'The thing is,' he complained, 'I can't do anything to encourage it to leave. This particular type sheds its hairs when it's frightened. They itch and hurt if you touch them, like nettles.'

'I think I've shed a few red hairs of my own. We've been keeping company for two hours and I have yet to scare *it*.' She looked down over the edge of her hammock at the top of Nic's head.

A quick movement caught her eye. 'It's moving! At least it's headed in the right direction. Yes!' he shouted and jumped up when the spider disappeared through the opening.

'What if it comes back? Still sleeping on the floor, Nic?' she asked, a gleam in her eyes.

His frantic gaze snagged on the wood pile beside the doorway. The Indians had brought it for them to keep their fire burning. Nic quickly restacked the wood against the opening, then sealed off the crack at the top with her shorts and shirt that she had hung on the twig.

'That reminds me,' she said, closing her book. 'Tomorrow's wash day. We need to have all our clothes clean before we start downriver. Put everything beside the door in the morning and I'll wash them. Is the runner still leaving tomorrow morning?'

He came back to the hammocks and, in the light, she was shocked to see how exhausted he looked.

He stretched then started to unbutton his shirt. 'At dawn. And I'm going hunting with the men tomorrow morning. We ate their food, so I'll help to replace it. We can head out after that. They say the rock formation is two days walk downriver by canoe. We can fly it in an hour.'

The medallion was the reason for this journey, and she had scarcely given it a thought since they started out. She understood that returning it meant more to her than to him, but this trip had been good for him, in many ways. It had given him back his sense of purpose, for one thing. It was right that he was here with her.

She took another hard look at him. His eyes were bright and the fruity, yeasty smell on his breath gave her a full feeling. 'What was that yellow drink they served?'

'A strong Indian beer made from honey. You mean you didn't try it?' His voice oozed skepticism.

'I only took a sip to be polite.' She clamped a hand over her mouth as she hiccuped softly at the recollection.

He laughed and came to stand in front of her. In the upper hammock where she sat cross-legged, she was level with his stomach.

'And look who's asking, anyway. How much did you really have, sitting back there where I couldn't keep an eye on that gourd they gave you?' he asked, eyes twinkling before his gaze moved down to her neck.

Gabby felt her heartbeat in the hollow of her throat. Nic's eyes lingering on it didn't help her control its pace.

'I've learned my lesson, thank you,' she said primly, desperate to change the atmosphere in the hut. 'I was afraid to drink it. Say, you didn't bring your cute little buddy home. I expected a house guest tonight, but not the eight-legged one.'

Nic's face lost all expression before he turned away, and his voice was flat when he spoke. 'He fell asleep in my lap. His mother took him.'

After a moment she asked gently, 'How old was your son, Nic?'

He slowly turned to her. 'So you know about him, do you? I wondered.'

She held his eyes. 'Paul mentioned your loss, before he realized I didn't know, then he wouldn't say anything more. I'm so sorry, Nic. You should have told me yourself.'

He started to pace around the hut, his eyes moving restlessly. 'He — He

159

was three,' he said in a strangely toneless voice, his back toward her. 'Now let's change the subject. I don't talk about it.'

Before she could utter another sound, she saw the trembling begin in his legs, working its way up through his body. Then his teeth began to chatter. She could have kicked herself for asking, when this awful pain came with his memories.

'Nic. Oh, Nic, forgive me. Me and my big mouth,' she said as she clambered out of her hammock. She ran to him in her unlaced boots, catching him up in a fierce embrace, willing her strength to stop the shuddering that tore through him.

'S-Sorry, Gabby,' he said, holding on to her just as fiercely. 'I'll be okay in a minute. I thought I was past this.'

'It's all right, Nic, just hang on tight,' she said, rocking him.

Gradually, the tremors ceased. She eased her hold on him slightly, stroking his back while she waited for him to let her know it was over.

He took a deep, shuddering breath then rested his chin on the top of her head. 'Will you be okay here if I sleep in the plane?' he asked carefully.

'I'll be fine, don't worry. Go on,' she said, giving him one last pat before she stepped away.

His face was white, his eyes full of pain when he looked down at her. 'Thanks, Gabby,' he whispered.

'Anytime, Nic,' she answered softly.

Before she could gather her thoughts, he unbarred the doorway and was gone. She stared after him a long time before she climbed into her hammock and eventually went to sleep.

At dawn she awoke to see Nic moving around the hut. 'What are you doing?' she mumbled. 'Are we leaving?'

'I'm bringing my laundry, as instructed. And thanks for doing it for me,' he said softly.

She mumbled a reply and closed her eyes. When she opened them again a minute later, it was to see him, through the gauzy mosquito netting, standing over her, his clenched fists resting on the edge of her hammock.

'I called him Nicky,' he began hesitantly. 'We named him Nicholas because she wouldn't use my Portuguese name.'

He paused and sighed. 'He was killed in a car accident two years ago. My ex-wife's new husband, or rather, her new victim, was driving. They weren't even hurt.

'We were married for two years and she was unfaithful the whole time, except for the first nine months, when she carried Nicky. At least I think she was faithful then. I know he was mine.'

She lay quietly looking up at him, with the mosquito netting between them like a confessional screen. He spoke about his son and his faithless marriage, his return to Brazil after the funeral, and his slow withdrawal from everyone and everything, except Luiz and the bar at the house.

'I never wanted to give a damn about

anybody or anything ever again. I built the walls around me thick and high and cold after I came back here. They were impenetrable. Being with you has made me remember, feel it all again. It hurts like hell, Gabby. What do I do now?' he finished quietly.

'You've already done it, Nic,' she said simply. 'You've started to live again.'

'I didn't think I remembered how.'

Her right hand slid out under the netting to cover one of his clenched fists. She felt it relax under her palm. 'Dad told me how it was with him after my mother died. He said life goes forward and you're along for the ride because you're still alive. Whether you steer or drift is up to you.'

He covered her hand, which still rested on his, with his other hand for a moment before he turned away. 'Go back to sleep. I'm going hunting with the headman and some of the men. See you tonight.'

Despite his sad visit, she did go back to sleep. When she got up, she washed their clothes in the stream beyond the bathing area. The children moved downstream to play in the mounds of bubbles her washing sent their way. She strung a line in the cargo area of the plane and hung the clothes there to dry, out of the way of any showers.

She finished just in time to join a small group of women and young girls going on a food gathering expedition into the forest. She jammed a sketchbook, some colored pencils, and a tiny set of folding binoculars into a knapsack, along with a small first aid kit she'd almost forgotten about.

They followed a narrow, shady trail to the garden plots belonging to each family. She circulated, trying to help each woman in turn, in any way she could. The plots apparently yielded little this time of year.

Thanks to her father she could identify most of the plants in them as plantains, manioc, and cotton plants for hammocks and the women's little apron coverings. Around the perimeter were scattered peach palms, papaya trees, sugar cane, maize, taro, yams, and cane for arrows. But the women's food baskets, attached to bark slings worn around their heads, were almost empty.

During a lull, Gabby sat down and made a quick sketch of an orchid that clung to a nearby tree. She had a whispering, gasping audience by the time she was finished. Shyly, the women touched the drawing. The young woman who had led her to the bathing pool yesterday leaned down to sniff it.

Bird calls and the sounds of other unseen rain forest life surrounded them. The women stopped their work once to listen to a sound they didn't recognize. She heard soft, nervous cries of, '*Curupira, Curupira,*' and they quickly moved on. Nic had explained that *Curupira* is a wild man, or spirit, of the forest who produces all noises the Indians are unable to explain.

They walked along a clearly marked trail with Gabby bringing up the rear. She watched some of them gingerly search out land crabs in their burrows near the roots of trees. When they opened a termite nest, sorting out the white grubs to be roasted and eaten, she nearly gagged and reminded herself to eat fruit for dinner that night.

A cry drew her attention away from the grubs. One of the girls, older sister to Nic's little shadow, had cut her palm on the sharp tool the women had used to open the nest.

The women gathered around her, chattering among themselves, while the girl, who looked to be around seven, sat on the ground nursing her hand. Gabby hesitated only a moment before gently pushing her way through the crowd and kneeling beside the girl.

The cut wasn't deep but it was bleeding profusely, which was good. Gabby smiled at the girl and touched her arm before reaching for her knapsack.

She searched the women's faces, looking for the older woman who seemed to be the leader of the group.

Making eye contact, she held up the first aid kit and made a giving motion toward the girl. The woman gave one curt nod of her head.

She had an avid audience as she poured hydrogen peroxide into the cut. To oohs and aahs she wiped away the resulting pink froth with cotton balls. Next she applied pressure with gauze until the bleeding stopped then packed the wound with antibiotic ointment. A clean gauze pad against the skin and white gauze wrapped around the girl's hand finished off her Florence Nightingale demonstration. Everybody was smiling when she left them to make her way back to the village alone.

The truth was, she wanted to sketch some more, and she preferred doing it alone. A little way off the trail she could see a giant tree that had fallen recently, clearing a path in its death fall. If she walked along its full length and returned the same way, that should satisfy Nic, since she couldn't possibly get lost.

Below her on the ground, as she walked on the tree's smooth bark, young trees and other plants were already jockeying for the places in the sunlight left by the fallen giant. She stopped every few feet and swept the area with the binoculars, to see what was growing there. When she reached the leafy top, she sat down and opened her sketchbook. There were orchids and cup-like bromeliads still clinging to the branches. She happily drew them.

Before she started back, she scanned the trees ahead. Suddenly a dazzling human smile filled her lenses. Startled, she regained her balance on the tree trunk and looked with her naked eyes at the high branch. An Indian man was sitting there. A friendly hunter? When she focused her binoculars on him, her stomach churned. It was a partially decomposed body, crawling with ants, tied to the tree. The smile was so dazzling because no flesh remained to frame its polished brightness.

She turned and ran blindly back

along the trunk. When she came to its exposed roots, she jumped down and plunged onto the trail without even slowing her headlong dash. She screamed when she ran up against a hard-muscled chest.

Nic's hands held her firmly around the waist. 'Where the hell have you been?' he spluttered, half in English, half in Portuguese. 'The women came back long ago. When you weren't with them, I — '

'Listen, Nic, there's a — ' she began, running her words together in her haste.

'Good!' He looked closely at her face. 'I hope something scared you witless out there,' he continued. 'What was it? Now will you stay in the village or at the bathing area until we leave?'

'Listen to me!' she shouted, slapping her sketchbook against his chest. 'There's a dead man tied in a tree back there!'

His reaction wasn't what she expected. He let go of her and he laughed. 'Sorry,' he said finally, his hands on his hips. 'It was the expression on your face.'

She felt her chin jut toward him. 'I'm glad you're so easily amused. What's so funny about a dead man tied to a tree?'

'Not a thing,' he said, still enjoying himself. 'I already know about your new friend. He died a couple of weeks ago. These Indians tie their dead in trees. In a few weeks there's nothing left but clean bones. They even tie the jaw on with a piece of vine that the ants can't chew through. Would you like to know what they do with the bones?'

'Spare me the details.' She tried to push past him but he put an arm around her waist and effortlessly pulled her around in front of him again.

'I'm not finished yet.' His voice was as cold and sharp as the deadly switchblade in his pocket. 'What the hell were you thinking of, playing doctor like that? You're the talk of the village.'

Puzzled, she asked, 'What's wrong? I asked permission from the older woman who — '

He cut her off. 'The only one whose permission matters around here in medical matters is the medicine man. And, man, is he pissed off.'

Her stomach lurched in fear. 'Oh. Well, what do you want me to do about it? Just tell me and I'll do it.' Her voice was rising in anger, too, and she couldn't stop it.

'Nothing! You've done quite enough, thank you. What if she gets an infection? What if he makes sure she does, to reinforce the lesson? How will the Amarals feel about my negotiations then? This could be as disastrous as that other D.O.'s accidental shooting, Gabby.'

She stared at him, letting the possible consequences of her seemingly harmless act of kindness crash around her. She caught her lower lip between her teeth when the last one settled. Nic's eyes moved to her mouth.

'I'm sorry,' she whispered.

He seemed to deflate, the tension leaving his body to droop in weariness. 'You were just being you. Stop it, will you?' he added with a half smile, stepping aside so she could go ahead of him on the path.

'What are you doing back so early, anyway?' she said over her shoulder.

'We ran into a wild boar and some monkeys not too far out. We got more than enough, so we came back. When I couldn't find you I — '

'*Deja vu*, Nic. Let's not go into that again.' She stopped and turned to him. 'I walked into the forest on a fallen tree. I walked out of the forest on the same fallen tree. I never left the stinking tree. How could I get lost?' She resumed her march to the village.

Sarcasm lay heavy in his next words. 'Silly me. So, I overreact a little when you disappear into the jungle alone.'

'Again. Like you did twelve years ago when I went outside the walls. *And* blazed a trail,' she added.

'Not quite like twelve years ago,' he said coldly. 'I didn't kiss you this time. And you didn't punch me in the stomach this time.'

She gave a very unladylike snort then ignored him. They went their separate ways when they reached the village.

Smarting from his laughter, hurting from his anger, and still spooked by her grisly discovery, she longed for something quietly domestic to concentrate on. First, though, she had to mend fences. Going to the plane, she checked her gear to see what goodies she could present to the medicine man, damn him, as a peace offering.

For starters she would give him the small first aid kit she had used on the girl. Kind of like handing over the reins, she told herself. Some nice tweezers, a spare set out of the big first aid kit, might suit. And a huge bottle of kids' bubble liquid. There was only one, so she hadn't given it to the children of either village.

'Let's see what the old goat makes of

these,' she muttered, gathering up the items and leaving the plane.

The circle of huts was quiet as she made her way to the medicine man's hut. She didn't know how to knock on a palm thatched wall and there wasn't any door, so she knelt a little distance away from the medicine man's open doorway, cleared her throat, and said 'Hello' loudly. When he appeared, she bent forward to touch her forehead on the ground. For Nic she would grovel.

Scowling, he sat down outside his door, daring her to dazzle him. Just when she decided this might not have been such a good idea, she became aware of a crowd gathering behind her.

Nothing in the first aid kit impressed him. He showed some interest in the tweezers after Gabby demonstrated their use by holding a tiny piece of wood between her fingers and plucking it out with them. When she held them out to him on both palms, he took them and grunted.

Cautiously she showed him the bottle

of bubbles, unscrewed the cap, and withdrew the plastic wand with the large ring at one end. She held it above her, against the light, and blew gently against the shiny film covering the wand's opening.

Squeals of delight from the crowd followed the iridescent globes skyward. She looked at the medicine man to gauge his reaction. He wore a sappy smile as he watched the last bubble float skyward. Bingo! She replaced the wand and cap and held the bottle out to him. He took it, actually laughing. She bowed again and retreated.

Back at their hut, she took a round of manioc bread from the basket of food brought to their doorstep that morning. As she ate, she put on her bikini and shirt. Sketchbook and colored pencils in hand, soap and shampoo in her pockets, and boots on her feet, she went to sit on the silver sand beach.

Some of the women and children who hadn't been at the bubble demo were bathing, but they politely left her alone. Her eyes followed the antics of the babies and children. They were sturdy little dark-eyed devils, laughing and playing all the time.

She picked up her sketchbook and soon she was surrounded by the children and their mothers. Apparently word of her ability to capture the rain forest on paper had spread among them. She hoped that was a good thing.

Two red and green Amazon kingfishers paused in their fishing until the human commotion ceased, giving her time to capture them on paper. Likewise, two blue and yellow macaws stopped for an argument on a branch on the other side of the pool and posed noisily for her. Brilliantly colored butterflies and patterned beetles kept her and her audience occupied for over an hour, then most of her companions deserted her.

Peeling off her shirt and kicking off her boots, she climbed onto the rock used as a diving off place by the children. Her body sliced the surface of the deep pool. The water felt silky and cool against her skin. She swam until she was tired then floated idly. Taking her shampoo from a rock, she lathered her hair and rinsed it by ducking under the water. Thinking of that shampoo commercial again, she bobbed to the surface, tossing her head back so that her hair threw off a fan of sparkling droplets in the sunlight. Climbing out of the pool, she leaned to one side and vigorously rubbed her wet waves and curls with her towel.

'A goddess rising from the sea,' Nic said softly from the forest path leading onto the beach.

Startled, she covered herself with her towel and glanced around. All the women and children were gone. They were alone, and she had the feeling Nic had been watching her for a while.

8

She tried to defuse the moment. 'Waxing poetic, Nic?'

He frowned. 'You sure know how to shoot down a compliment, Gabby.'

She defended herself. 'It's self defense. I work in a world of Brazilian men.'

His shirt was unbuttoned and he carried his towel in his hand. 'I came down earlier but you looked like the old woman who lived in a shoe. The kids were three-deep around you.'

She relaxed and returned his smile. 'I was sketching. They were fascinated.'

'They think you make strong magic. I thought I was the only one you bewitched. Now I know you bewitch everyone. That medicine man is purring like a kitten and still blowing bubbles.' He grinned crookedly.

'You saw?' Her face was on fire right

up to her hairline. 'I was trying to placate him for your sake.'

'You did. Thanks.' He hesitated. 'I want to apologize. I shouldn't have yelled at you or laughed when you were upset. I'm sorry.' He walked toward her. 'I worry about you. I won't apologize for that.'

'Hey, I'm not used to anyone worrying about me anymore. Give me some time to get used to it.'

'Besides that,' he added, with a big grin, 'if something happens to you while you're with me, it means weeks and weeks of paperwork.'

She sent him a quelling look. 'Your apologies are unique, I'll say that for them. I'll try not to die while we're together, okay? Besides, you came upriver with me.' She squeezed more water out of her hair with her towel.

His brows drew down in a frown while he began a slow, meticulous look at her. 'Don't even go there, Gabby. You better hope my boss never finds out just how I came to be in *your* tender care.'

'Stop staring, Nic,' she snapped. 'You're not sixteen anymore.' Turning away, she brought the towel around her sarong-style and tucked in the end.

'We've had this conversation already. Neither of us is sixteen anymore. That's why I'm staring. Don't tell me a man has never looked at you like this before.' His voice was quite close now. 'I'm imagining what you could do for a *tanga*, Rio's micro-bikini.'

She turned to face him, surprised at just how close he was. 'I know what a *tanga* is, thank you. And I don't own one.'

'Pity,' he said, folding his long body down onto the sand at her feet and picking up her sketchbook. 'Hey, these are really good.'

She sat down beside him. 'I still enjoy sketching when I see something worthy of the effort.'

He flipped through the pages, pausing when he came to his own face, sucking in his breath when his father looked back at him from a page, then her own father.

He didn't speak again until he got to a drawing of the medallion. 'I'd forgotten how beautiful it is. It's no wonder my dad couldn't resist it. He convinced your dad that they should take it, you know. That's why they fell out later.'

She nodded. The sketches of their fathers and the medallion brought back in a rush the reason she was there. A sense of urgency came with it. It hadn't rained a lot over the past few days. It wouldn't hold off much longer.

'Let's go, Nic. Now,' she said in a rush. 'If we don't find the formation before dark, we can pick a sandbar and sleep in the plane or make camp. We could return the medallion tomorrow and start downriver.'

His eyes slid away from the sketch to her face. 'In the plane, we'd probably reach the rock formation in an hour or so.' They both looked up at the sun and the clouds rolling in. 'How long would it take you to pack up?'

'Half an hour. Tops.'

'You're on. Bring my stuff and I'll meet you at the plane. Leave the soap and shampoo. I want to clean up before we go.'

They worked around the lines of wet clothes in the cargo area of the plane to refuel, using the last of the drums of fuel. During rest stops along the way upriver, though it went against their beliefs, they had off-loaded their empties to lighten the plane so they could get every mile out of every drop of fuel. They moved the last of the empty drums close to the cargo doors.

'After this, we paddle or we walk,' Nic said, coiling the hose onto a hook.

'We can fly downriver until we're dry,' Gabby said.

He frowned, watching her as she moved around, checking the tiedowns on everything. 'We'll have to see how the river behaves. If the formation is where I think it is, I saw plenty of rapids and we can't land there. We might have to fly past the rapids and walk back to the rock ledge.'

'I think we have everything we need for the river leg of the journey.' She walked toward the back of the plane. 'Paddles, the raft, dehydrated food, canteens. All we have to add is the tent, medical kit, and our sleeping gear. I even have a deck of cards in there somewhere.' She absently fingered the medallion which she had placed around her neck, she hoped, for the last time.

'Is everything the way you want it back here?' he asked. When she nodded, he continued, 'Then let's say our good-byes and get on with it.'

Nic gave the little boy a hug and a stray coin from his pocket before they left the village. He seemed more relaxed with the boy, she noticed.

The medicine man made a brief appearance to give her a bracelet made out of seeds. The presentation smacked of one expert paying respect to another.

As a result of her short time with the two Indian groups, she had a new respect for these people of the rain forest. She admired the ingenuity and dignity with which they lived their lives in this inhospitable environment, an environment that let man know he was not welcome here. She was impressed with their uses of the many plants available to them. She smiled when she realized that she was her father's daughter after all.

Casually observing the two groups, she had seen them extract a bitter form of salt from water hyacinths, make a primitive form of birth control by distilling the passion flower, which Nic told her stopped ovulation, and use the strychnos vine for curare on their darts and arrows.

She smiled when she noticed a string of bubbles heading skyward as they walked back to the plane.

When they climbed aboard, she took the pilot's seat. 'I'll take the controls today. You, Mr. Geologist, know what we're looking for.'

'That's good, because it will be on

my side of the plane,' he said, buckling his seat belt and starting the pre-flight check. 'Follow the river. We can't afford to miss it.'

The rain came down steadily while the river looped and turned on itself. When it finally unkinked, its surface was broken by stretches of rapids. Nic called out when a beckoning finger of dark rock poked out of the jungle below.

He scanned the white water surrounding it. 'Like I said, rapids up, down, and all around.'

The roiling, boiling waters beneath their wings left her no choice. 'Let's go on downriver. We can walk back.'

In a couple of minutes a smooth, deep pool appeared below them, sandwiched between the formation's rapids and a second, rougher set.

'You're going for it?' Nic asked in amazement as she circled the pool.

Gabby was intent on picking the right spot within the pool and then putting the plane into it. 'I've landed and taken off in The Duck from smaller.'

'Well, don't ditch us here. Every minute in the air shortens our days of paddling and dodging all the stuff floating in the river. Be careful, Gabby.'

'I'm always careful, Nic. Relax. And I'm always calm during rough landings and takeoffs. Used to drive my instructors crazy.' Her voice sounded dreamy even to her own ears.

'I know the feeling.' She felt him look at her briefly then look back again. 'Damn it, Gabby, don't fall asleep on me.'

'Shut up, Nic.'

She set The Duck down gently on the surface and taxied toward the spot she'd picked on shore. Without warning the plane rocked wildly, accompanied by a thump as something in the water came in contact with one of the floats.

'Oops.'

'I hate that word, especially from a pilot,' he said through clenched teeth. 'You should have cross hairs painted on your windshield.'

They secured the plane with extra ropes then examined the float. It was damaged but not enough to keep them from continuing downriver the next day.

Nic looked at the sky, which had started to clear a little. 'Let's take the gear and set up camp on the ledge. We have a couple of hours of daylight left to look for the shrine.'

She divided the equipment and food loads between their packs while Nic hacked an opening into the forest. Once they were through the thick foliage along the river's edge, they could walk quickly along the almost-clear forest floor. It didn't take long to reach the formation.

'Look at the size of that thing,' Nic said in awe as they approached the high, rippled rock thrusting up out of the forest floor. 'Dad must have loved this.'

Gabby developed an active cluster of Amazonian butterflies in her stomach when she first saw the formation up close. The moment was so near, the culmination of a lot of soul-searching, hard work, and lost time on her part.

'It seems to me his son appreciates it, too,' she said as they put down their packs.

Nic easily climbed the five feet of rock wall, and she handed everything up to him. Then he bent his knees slightly and reached down to her with both hands. 'Grab my forearms.'

When her grip satisfied him, he wrapped his fingers around her forearms, braced his feet, and pulled. She got purchase on the rock with the toes of her boots, but mostly it was his strength that pulled her up to him.

The sensation left her breathless. She looked into his face, hanging on to him even when her feet were firmly on the rock in front of his boots. When he returned her look, she blinked once.

His eyebrows briefly leapt into his forehead. 'You fly the way you do and you were afraid I'd drop you five feet?'

She mentally shook herself and let go of his muscled forearms. 'Well, I'm really glad you didn't because I don't bounce like I did when I was a kid.'

'If I'd known that I *would* have dropped you. Jungle Eyes,' he added as he turned away and started erecting the tent.

They set up the camp hurriedly. She unpacked the last of the canned food and a tiny propane stove she'd brought for the times it wasn't convenient to make a conventional fire. They gathered up Nic's machete and rifle and her flashlight and started inland on the formation.

As usual, Nic took the lead. She stayed behind him but to his right so she, too, could see ahead. The climb was slight but steady.

Moss covered the surface of the rock, making it slippery in spots. Ferns and other plants had footholds in every crevice, and the giant trees grew close, converging above to form a covered walkway. The plants' roots had already begun the eons-long task of cleaving the stone into smaller boulders. Nic paused several times where the rock was exposed to look more closely at it.

Finally, he stopped and turned to her. 'We'd better turn back for tonight.'

'What if we don't find it tomorrow, Nic?' She heard apprehension in her voice.

He shrugged. 'We'll build our own shrine and put the medallion inside. Don't worry about it.'

She stood looking after him when he turned back the way they had come. She didn't want to build a new shrine, but she would if they couldn't find the original one. It would at least fulfill the spirit of their mission and she hoped that would be enough.

In the next moment, she realized how thankful she was that he was with her. He was back in her life again and she didn't want to leave him behind when she left Brazil. What would he think if he figured that out, she wondered?

It took only a few minutes to heat the

cans of food on the propane stove, and they managed to get everything cleaned up and put away before it started to rain again. By the light of the pressure lamp they played poker, rummy, and war for a couple of hours, sitting Indian-style on their mats and blankets inside the tent.

'So, you have plans when we get back?' he asked as he swept up the cards to shuffle them.

These new, confusing feelings she'd discovered for Nic made her unsure of the plans she had made, so she spoke hesitantly.

'After I sell my amphibian, I'll go back to the States. I can get my pilot's license there, maybe even be an instructor. And I have some distant cousins that I might look up.'

'And find your 'nice man.' Don't forget him,' he added.

I think I already found him, she told herself, but to him she said brightly, 'I live in hope. In Brazil I've been propositioned more than proposed to.'

'I'll bet you have.' He smiled but kept his eyes on the deck as he cut it. 'Do you really think you'll be content with a quiet life?'

'And just who said my life will be quiet?' she asked indignantly. 'I'm going to have a big house in the country with a little face looking out each window and another one on the way.'

Nic had been doing a fancy shuffle and abruptly a fountain of cards flicked into the air to float down all over the inside of the tent. She watched them settle quietly around them like falling leaves. He was staring at her when she looked at him, laughing.

'If that was a card trick, Nic, it needs practice.' She started to gather up the cards.

He looked embarrassed. 'No. No, it was . . . what you said.'

She patted the cards she held into a neat pile. 'Sorry if I shocked you, but I just turned 27 and I want to start my family.'

'You didn't embarrass me. It's just that . . . '

She was on all fours and looked at him over her shoulder when his voice trailed off. 'You feel the same way yourself.' It wasn't a question.

He nodded, not looking at her, and scooped up more cards. 'I did. Once.'

She sat back on her heels. 'I think it was our upbringing, Nic. I want my babies to have lots of brothers and sisters to laugh with, fight with, cry with. I won't raise lonely children.' She handed him the cards.

'You've grown up to be an unusual woman, Gabby, different from any other woman I've ever met.'

'Thank you. I think.' She picked up a card that lay on her blanket, the ace of hearts, and sailed it to him. 'Enough of this. Let's go to bed.' When he went very still and she caught his confused look, she amended quickly, 'Let's go to *sleep* now, Nic.'

She brought her basin in out of the rain to wash her face and hands.

Smiling to herself, she watched as Nic put his rifle between the sleeping mats this time. There was no way he could get past that to snuggle up to her in the night, she thought.

He proved her wrong.

She woke the next morning feeling nervy and out of sorts. It was hot and stuffy in the tent. She lay still for a moment, looking at the roof and listening to the rushing river, until she became aware of an unaccustomed weight. She looked down over herself then over at Nic.

He sprawled on his stomach beside her. His right forearm lay up along her side and his right hand rested on her left breast. She wondered what had happened to his rifle. By turning her head and looking up, she could see its stock resting parallel to the top of her mat.

She was studying his sleeping face when he finally stirred. Quickly she looked back to the tent ceiling and waited.

He swore quietly in Portuguese then lifted his hand and arm away.

'I wonder if the plane is all right,' she said by way of 'good morning.'

He froze for a second at the sound of her voice. Pushing himself up, he turned around into a sitting position, then pulled on his socks, boots, and shirt. 'Sorry, Gabby,' he said simply, followed by, 'Coffee,' as he crawled out of the tent.

'Amen,' she agreed and followed him.

They ate cheese and crackers accompanied by lots of coffee and silence. Later, neither of them spoke as they left camp and retraced their steps, walking side by side along the formation.

It wasn't a companionable silence, although they walked close together. Nic had closed the gates and pulled up the drawbridge. At Gabby's place the lights were on but nobody was home. She kept her eyes down while purpose drove her steps.

Nic suddenly stopped. Gabby was a full pace ahead of him before she realized it. She turned to look at him then followed the direction of his gaze.

Ahead, centered on the rock formation, was a small, moss-covered structure. After four hundred years its shape was still discernible, although plants clung to it and blurred its lines.

She slowly moved toward it, taking for granted that Nic was right behind her. The shrine came up to her waist, a simple pyramid-shaped cavern of well-stacked stones. When she looked more closely, she saw that the plants and their roots had reinforced the shrine rather than weakened it. A white orchid, like an offering, grew at the base of the opening.

Beside the shrine, indistinguishable until she stood before it, were little mossy elevations, bumps, and one rounded hump. She knew instinctively they were the corroded, delicate pieces of metal her father had carefully laid out twelve years ago to form the rough shapes of the Spaniard's breast-plate and helmet. A wave of missing him washed over her and she held her breath against the pain.

Nic's tense voice called her back. 'You are not putting your hand in there. We'll find some way of getting the medallion inside, but you're not — '

'Whatever you say, Nic,' she interrupted in a tiny, submissive voice.

She almost missed the look of surprise he shot at her. She dropped to her knees, took the medallion from around her neck, and removed the rawhide shoelace she'd used for a chain.

'Can you crack the clay off without damaging the medallion?' Her voice shook.

Whatever he saw in her face and eyes when she looked up at him made him rock slightly on his feet. He hooked his rifle sling off his shoulder and knelt beside her then searched in his pockets for a handkerchief. He found two. Gabby produced two also. When the medallion was double padded, top and bottom, he hit it with the butt of the rifle.

The artist friend she had asked to cover the medallion had layered rice paper to protect the gold. The clay cracked and fell away in large pieces. The paper peeled off, leaving the gold and its carvings clean and shining. She used her shirttail to buff the medallion one last time.

There were three figures in the center of the sunburst, a tiny bird twisting in flight, a sturdy, full-throated howler monkey staring solemnly, and a jaguar, long and lithe, leaping toward unseen prey. Surrounding them in a glorious halo, the sunrays burst outward around them.

'You can use the flat of the rifle stock to put it inside,' Nic said, checking the safety then offering her the gun, butt first.

'No. Not the rifle, Nic. It doesn't seem right.'

He sighed and sat back on his heels like an Indian. 'What then?'

'Some leaves? A branch?' She shrugged.

He unearthed a forked branch and she found a broad, flexible leaf. They used a piece of the rawhide shoelace to tie the leaf across the fork, creating a paddle.

When it was ready, Gabby patted the rock beside her. 'Come on, Nic.'

He towered over her like one of the rain forest giants around them. 'This is your show, Gabby, not mine.'

'Please, Nic? It's not a show and it's ours to do together. If you won't do it for me, then do it for your dad's memory.'

'You'll use anything, shamelessly, to manipulate me, won't you?' he grumbled, giving her a lopsided grin.

'Shut up, Nic,' she said fondly.

He knelt down beside her, muttering. Reverently, she placed the medallion on the leaf paddle and extended it toward the shrine's opening. With her free hand she took Nic's right hand and placed it over her own on the branch. She put her left arm around him and inched closer to him.

The branch trembled then steadied as it passed over the orchid to deposit its sacred cargo inside the shrine. Nic quickly took his hand away and stood up, watching quietly as she turned the paddle around and used the end to straighten the medallion inside. The gold seemed to glow with an inner light within the dark opening.

'Are we absolved and 'normal' now that we've returned it?' he asked, shrugging the rifle sling over his shoulder.

'It's official,' she said lightly, around the lump in her throat.

'Come on, Gabby, let's go home.' He turned toward the river.

'Okay, Nic.'

She got to her feet to follow him, pausing for just a moment to look back. 'Well, at last it's done, Dad,' she whispered then hurried to catch up.

9

They broke camp in the rain. When they got back to where they left the plane, they had to wade out to it because the river had risen a foot. They tied their boot laces together and draped the boots around their necks to keep the important footwear dry. Their packs were light and small enough that only one trip was necessary.

'Who flies, Nic? Short ride,' she said after they stowed the gear and secured everything.

'You. You're a better pilot in a tight situation.' Before she had time to purr over the compliment, he added, 'But please, don't crash land. I'm not in the mood.'

'I wish I could have brought more fuel. I hate the thought of leaving her.' She patted the plane's side as she made her way forward.

Nic followed. 'Do you realize it would have been easier to fly in from Colombia or Venezuela than up the Sonhos?'

'Yes, I do, but *I* was in Sao Paulo and *you* were on the Sonhos,' she explained.

'Remind me to move.'

'So, move, Nic.' She fought the breathlessness that came with her next words. 'Come with me to the States. We'll start our own air service.'

'Hamilton and O'Hara? Hey, I like it,' he said, smiling.

The crumpled float gave her a little trouble during takeoff. With the water level rising, the Sonhos covered the beginning of the rapids, giving her a few hundred feet to compensate for the drag of the damaged float. After they were airborne, she watched the fuel gauge carefully. They weren't in the air very long when the engine coughed. She wanted to believe that The Duck, with no cargo except themselves and a light load of supplies, gave her the extra miles as a parting gift.

Nic was asleep and, for the sake of his nerves, she decided to let him sleep through the landing, since it wasn't a very good stretch of river. There weren't any rapids and it was deep enough but flotsam of all sizes and shapes dotted the water. She checked to see if he still had his seat belt fastened. He did.

The engine coughed again, meaning it this time. They were landing on fumes.

She admitted to herself that it wasn't the smoothest landing she ever made, but there really wasn't any reason for Nic to sit bolt upright and complain of whiplash.

The engine was sputtering regularly now and she pointed the nose toward a spit of sandbar still visible above the dark water. They stopped abruptly when the floats sliced into the sand.

'I will personally paint those cross hairs on your windshield when we get back, *if* we get back,' Nic ground out, his jaws tightly clenched.

'Hey, I missed all those floating trees,

didn't I?' She grinned at him but got no response. 'Remember what our dads used to say? 'Any landing you can walk away from is a good one.' '

Nic humored her and helped her tie The Duck to two trees with ropes that they slung as high up the trunks as they could manage. She was grateful to him but, at the same time, could have kicked him for all the things he could be saying but wasn't.

He eventually grew tired of watching her fuss with the tethers. 'Face it, Gabby, the movement of the water will probably smash her to pieces against the trees anyway. And there's no chance of your coming back to retrieve her, unless,' he stressed, 'you fly down from the north.'

'I know,' she answered raggedly, her resentment gone.

Truly saying good-bye to The Duck hurt more than she thought it would. For a moment she couldn't breath over the pain. It must have shown on her face because Nic patted her awkwardly on the back. She turned her attention to their preparations.

They inflated the sturdy, two-man raft and unloaded the supplies they needed from the plane into it, carefully distributing the weight. Just as she had planned, they weren't carrying a heavy or bulky load. It stopped raining by the time they pushed off from the sandbar and sat down on the plastic seats, bow and stern. With dry eyes, only just, she turned around for a last look at The Duck then kept her eyes ahead on the unfriendly river.

As kids they had gone on many short river trips in a dugout canoe, as well as in bigger canoes on longer trips with their fathers. They had camped out alone a few times, too, but always close to the house. Life on the river, especially this river in this mood, was going to be more uncomfortable than she remembered it. With grim determination she grasped the lightweight aluminum paddle and plunged it into the dark water of the Rio Sonhos, falling into a rhythm of using it off the right side of the bow seat.

Now that they were on the river, they saw more floating objects than they had seen from the air, especially trees. Nic, who did the steering with his paddle, worked hard to stay clear of them. With the speed of the river and their paddling, they shot downstream at an amazing rate.

The sky cleared and the sun gained strength rapidly. Soon perspiration streamed down her face and her clothing stuck to her skin as the devastating glare and increasing humidity sucked moisture from her body. Her shoulders began to ache relentlessly and after a few hours her hands were stinging and burning.

'Are we stopping soon?' she asked hoarsely.

'Not unless you need a bathroom stop. We'll go straight through until late this afternoon because we're covering more distance than I expected. Just keep drinking from the canteens and take some salt pills with it. We can eat what's left of the fresh fruit without stopping.'

At one point, she twisted around to offer him some chewing gum, taking a stick herself to help relieve her intense thirst. She had pulled her hat lower over her eyes and put on her sunglasses. Nic wore a wide-brimmed bush hat with a jaguar band that Luiz had tucked in his pack. He looked good enough to eat, she decided before she turned back to her paddling.

The water now resembled strong tea with a little milk added as it swept them past shoreline that was as varied as the birds and animals they saw. The river's edges changed from rocky beaches, to sandy beaches, to solid walls of green, to brown banks, to sandbanks, to sandbars. They moved swiftly and silently on the river that was rising steadily from the rains.

Their quiet approach allowed them to see wildlife that would ordinarily have fled. Pony-sized tapirs, rodent-like capybaras, and peccaries, the roasted wild pig of Indian feasts, dashed away from them, outraged at being surprised as they drank.

When they rested, they allowed the swift current to carry them along, with Nic dipping his paddle to correct their direction. He had to be constantly vigilant against the fallen trees that moved downstream like battering rams, sometimes on both sides of them. At times he turned around to face the river, when they were in an especially thick flow of them, and maneuvered the raft closer to the riverbank.

Sometimes she cheated and stopped paddling just to watch the birds. Colorful hummingbirds flitted among splashes of equally colorful flowers, while red and blue macaws, and green parrots and parakeets decorated the trees, filling the air with their calls. Once from deep in the forest came a single, metallic peal that sounded like someone was striking a bell.

'Nic, a bellbird!' she said, listening raptly.

Bellbirds had been her favorite when she was new to the rain forest, and it was a sound from her childhood that she still welcomed into her dreams at night.

'A little less enthusing and a lot more paddling would be much appreciated,' he said so coldly that she swung around to look at him. His hat was pulled down low and his gray-blue eyes burned in the shadow of its brim like an animal looking out of a cave.

She quickly and quietly turned back to her paddling. From the look on his face she realized that now was not the time to ask what had set him off.

They entered a relatively quiet stretch of river where groups of monkeys chattered in the trees and occasionally threw things at them. A caiman, six or seven feet long, slid silently into the water from a sandbank lined with short, flood-scoured tree trunks, watching them with cold, cruel eyes. She'd forgotten how much she feared the South American crocodile. Unexpectedly, several of the 'tree trunks' on the sandbank sprouted legs and crashed into the water, making her jump. She sensed rather than saw Nic reach for his rifle. She resumed her paddling with renewed energy until they left the sandbank of 'tree trunks' far behind.

In the afternoon the skies unexpectedly opened and drenched them with stinging rain while the sun still beat down.

'A shower massage!' Gabby laughed and turned her face and her palms up to the sky.

'This shower massage can swamp us. Get a cooking pot and start bailing,' Nic shouted over the roar of the rain.

Soon the sky darkened and there was vicious thunder and lightning. The sheets of rain striking the surface of the river and the accompanying mist forced Gabby's world to shrink to the bottom of the raft and her frantic bailing. It ended almost as abruptly as it had begun.

On her hands and knees, she looked up at Nic, wiping her streaming face and laughing. He smiled grimly and poured the water out of his hat brim over the side.

He pushed them until there was only an hour of daylight left. Then he searched out a little stream, not much wider than the raft, that flowed into the Sonhos. The only indication of it she could see from the river was a slight indentation in the green wall of riverbank.

Nic carefully changed places with her in the raft. With his newly sharpened machete, which he now wore on his belt, he slashed through the thick growth then maneuvered the raft through the rough opening. The banks of the stream were at chest level as they paddled up it to make camp for the night. It was like paddling through a green tunnel within the forest's shade.

When she stepped out of the raft, Gabby staggered. Weakness washed over her, nearly bowling her over. Nic grabbed her arm to steady her then shoved a banana into her hand.

'Here, eat this and drink some more water. It's just low blood sugar and maybe a little dehydration.' His voice was cold.

He could say what he liked. *She* knew when she had been hit by a truck. Her knees gave way and she simply sat down where she was. Then she lay back, closing her eyes against the dizziness that assailed her and clutching the banana to her chest.

'Why are you doing this?' Her hurt feelings were loud and clear in the rasping words. 'It isn't an endurance test, you know. More payback? When I'm eighty, I suppose you'll tamper with the brakes on my wheelchair then scream 'Remember the Sonhos!' at me as I roll past out of control.'

He stomped over to where she lay, kneeling on one knee beside her. 'No, this situation is too serious for simple payback.'

He took hold of her shirt collar and slowly pulled her to a sitting position, bringing on a new wave of dizziness. 'Didn't you see that river today — and what's in it. 'Oh, Nic, a bellbird! Oh, Nic, a shower massage!' ' he mimicked in a highpitched voice. Then it sank to a deep male shout. 'Oh, Gabby, honkin' big floating trees that can capsize us. And giant caiman just to make it really interesting.

'Damn it, Gabby, I let you talk me into this because you *cried*, one of the oldest tricks in the female arsenal, that and getting pregnant, and I *fell* for it, like a green teenager.' He let go of her and she fell back, a puppet whose strings had been cut.

She moaned, closing her eyes again as the trees spun around her. 'Don't assign *her* tactics to me, mister. And as for my female arsenal, well, if I have one, I don't know where I keep it. I didn't sob against your manly chest, you know. It was one stinking tear that slipped past because of something that really mattered to me. Oh, go to hell, Nic. Or better yet, just shoot me. I'm too tired to live.'

'Don't tempt me!'

He paid no attention to her after that, muttering to himself as he paced back and forth beside where she lay. 'We covered a lot of river today, and I'm going to get us back to Grilo as fast as I can. We can radio for a plane from there. We'll see how the river looks tomorrow. Hell, it would be safer to walk out through the rain forest than ride that river, even if it would take longer.'

When she opened her eyes, the trees were standing still, even if Nic wasn't. 'You're a pig, Nic,' she observed.

'So you've told me many, many times before. Eat that banana and you'll feel better. We have things to do,' he growled.

'I know I've said it before, but you keep refining and improving upon your . . . pigness. With age you've become an unsympathetic, unfeeling, chauvinist pig, Nic.'

Suddenly he knelt, ripped the banana's skin off in one vicious tear right under her nose and before her astonished eyes, then shoved the fruit into her gaping mouth.

She glared at him while she chewed. Her next words came out muffled around a mouthful of fruit. 'And do you know what you can do with the rest of those bananas?'

'Surprise me.' He stood up and nudged her gently with his foot. 'Get up. We're losing the light.'

As much as she hated to admit it, he was right about her blood sugar. She felt better after she finished the banana, took more salt pills, and sipped some water.

In a silence that neared the breaking point, they unloaded what they needed out of the raft and set up camp. She put some dehydrated stew into a pot with water from a canteen and set it on the propane stove to simmer. While she did that, Nic refilled the canteens from the stream and put water treatment tablets into each.

'I'm going upstream to wash my hair and have a bath.' She kept her voice chilly and distant.

After she gathered up what she needed, she took another banana from the bunch, slid it into her shirt pocket, and stalked away, letting her feelings show in her stiff, squared shoulders.

The little stream grew narrower the farther she went. The water in it still ran clear, she noted. That meant this was probably an underground spring that surfaced somewhere in the rain forest. Deep in thought and kicking things as she went, she walked too far and had to backtrack to a spot just right for her purposes.

She stripped down to her lacy bra and no-nonsense cotton underwear and visited a tree before clambering down the bank. Since she planned to rinse them out anyway, it wouldn't matter if her underthings got wet.

A nice flat rock conveniently poked itself up out of the middle of the stream. She waded out to it to sit with her feet and legs in the water while she ate her banana.

Immediately, tiny fish, so thin they were almost invisible, crowded around her legs. She wouldn't have seen them except that the fading light flashed off their sides as they darted frantically this way and that. She sat there playing with them, actually feeling them touching her skin and hands.

Suddenly Nic's voice echoed all around her. 'Get out! Get out of the water, Gabby!' She could hear his booted feet pounding on the earth like thunder as he ran upstream toward her.

She screamed and leaped to the bank then scrambled to its top, looking wildly around her for the danger. She punched her nerveless hands into the sleeves of her shirt and pulled it tightly around her. Electric eels, caiman, jaguars, and snakes that could squeeze the life out of her flashed through her mind while her feet remained stubbornly rooted to the spot.

Nic appeared, shirtless and wild-eyed, to skid to a halt in front of her. '*Candiru*! Were you — ? Did you sit in the water?'

She felt her head jerk in acknowledgment. 'O-On that rock. M-My feet and legs. I splashed a little over myself. W-What's *candiru*?'

His vicious-sounding spat of Portuguese ended in a moan. He took her face between his hands, looking into her eyes. She saw fear in his. 'Did you sit in the water . . . without your underwear?' he asked carefully, something in his voice barely in check. 'Did you relieve yourself while you were in the water?'

She was suddenly dumb with terror. What awful thing lurked in the clear, sparkling water? And why hadn't he unsheathed the now razor-sharp machete at his waist to do something about it?

When she mutely shook her head,

she saw his body sag, limp with relief, as he let go of her. 'Are you sure?'

'I'm sure. W-What's *candiru*?' she repeated, the word sounding familiar now.

'I told you about them a long time ago. Don't you remember?' he said gently, his voice shaking. '*Candiru* are tiny fish that gather in schools around a naked human in shallow water. They wriggle deep into delicate parts of the body, male or female, and lodge themselves there by extending two spines. They feed on blood and they have to be cut out. They'll follow a stream of urine back to its source.'

As the meaning of his words sank in, she let go of the edges of her shirt. Her mouth opened and closed but no words came out as she stared at him in painful, horrified silence, remembering the feel of the tiny fish against her fingers. An endless list of catastrophes that could happen to them out here slashed through her mind and she felt the blood drain from her face.

Finally, one Portuguese slang word came out clearly and in a quite ordinary tone of voice. It was the most terrible, dreadful word she had ever heard, in any language, from the men she worked with. A word whose meaning wasn't even clear to her. A word Nic *hadn't* shouted into the radio a lifetime ago. A word she had never spoken before in her life.

Then she gave a small, terrified whimper and threw her arms around his neck, catching a glimpse of Nic's face in a frozen moment of astonishment before she buried her face against the warm skin of his shoulder.

Now it was her turn to be held and comforted as she trembled. His arms came around her, lifting her off her feet. She felt his laughter, weak but irresistible, getting past his shock at her fall from grace.

'Y-You didn't make them up. When we were kids, I thought you made them up to sc-scare me,' she said in a tiny voice.

'No, I didn't make them up. Why do you think I taught you to use trees?' Nic said in a choked voice. 'There's no need to make up anything. We have it all out here.'

After a while she said against his warm, comforting skin. 'I'm so sorry, Nic, for everything. For not listening to you, for what I did to you, for dragging you into this. If — When — we get back to the house, you can arrest me if you want to. I'll go quietly. And I hear a rubber hose doesn't leave any marks. Or you can kick my female arsenal the whole way home, and I won't say a word, I promise.'

His laugh then his voice rumbled beneath her cheek. 'Trust me, Gabby, arresting you or beating you with a rubber hose are two things I haven't thought about doing to you for a long time now.' He set her on her feet but didn't let go of her. She became aware of their skin touching from waist to chest, nothing between them except her bra.

'I shouldn't do what I'm about to do. I apologize in advance,' he said wearily, explaining it to himself at the same time. 'But I'm exhausted. Wiped out. Physically, mentally, emotionally. And kissing you senseless is the only relief I see in sight.'

Not sure she had heard him correctly, she raised her head to look up at him. 'What?'

It took her only a second to realize she *had* heard him correctly. She expected the punishing pressure of his earlier kisses at the Amaral village, exciting though they had been. This time, however, his feather soft movements against her lips with his own were so gentle that she leaned into him.

Standing between his boots, she felt her toes curl into the soft earth of the riverbank, until she slowly rose up onto them, feeling the soft hair on his chest sliding against her bare skin. Every one of her senses clamored at the sensations flooding through her. Her hands slipped up over the smooth skin of his shoulders and neck in a slow caress. She could have sworn the whole forest rocked as she gave as good as she got.

He swore quietly and put her away from him. She stared at him as the air between them vibrated with a force that made the tiny hairs on her body stand on end. Never in her life had she kissed or been kissed like that, leaving her whole body buzzing with a warm hum.

Before she could gather the few wits she had left to her, he kissed the tip of her nose and told her to put on her boots. Still shaky, she felt his intense look as he held her arm to steady her. Then, wordless, she stumbled along behind him as he pulled her by her hand toward their camp.

The only words he uttered were, 'The food is ready.'

When they got back to the fire, he made her sit down in front of him and hold out her hands, palms up. He dug in the first aid kit for antiseptic, antibiotic cream, and cotton balls.

He wouldn't meet her eyes. 'Tell me about any cuts, scratches, or sores anywhere on your body. You know as well as I do that you can get a raging infection in a few hours in this climate.'

He gently dabbed at the raw places on her palms, their earthshaking kiss apparently forgotten, while she could still scarcely put two words together.

She remembered what he said before he kissed her. For him, now, it never happened. It was simply a release after a tiring, nerve crunching day. Despite what she felt, which she was afraid to examine too closely, she had no choice but to play it his way.

Too weary even to speak after that, they ate their stew, tidied the camp, and crawled into the tent. Her head was pounding, so she took some aspirin and jammed the bottle into her shorts pocket, too tired to put it back inside the first aid box.

As her eyes closed, she watched Nic put his rifle, his machete, and his boots between their sleeping mats. Yet, when she woke up briefly the next morning, her hand was nestled in Nic's, on top of his rifle and his machete and his boots. She laced her fingers with his and went back to sleep.

10

First thing the next morning, Nic walked down along the edge of the stream to study the river through the opening he had cut through the vegetation.

He answered her questioning look in a grim voice. 'It's worse. We have to weigh the advantage of the distance we'll gain with the risks of the river. What do you want to do?'

She thought over her answer while she dumped packets of cereal into boiling water for breakfast. Nic obviously wanted to end this enforced togetherness with her as quickly as possible. Their childhood friendship would always be part of both of them, but it was different now. After he thought about it, if he thought about it at all, he probably felt like he had kissed his sister yesterday.

'You want to get to Grilo ASAP; I want to get out of Brazil ASAP.' She stopped and looked up at him. 'But you're the expert so it's your call.'

His features went unreadable. 'We'll take our chances one more day on the river. After that it'll be suicidal. If we change our minds, we can get off the river and take it from there.'

While she finished breakfast, Nic neatly wrapped their paddle handles with special leaves, tying them on with pieces of vine. She remembered her dad showing her the plant and telling her its leaves had soothing juices. She noticed that Nic had raw places on his hands, too.

The sky was overcast when they shot out of the tiny stream onto the Sonhos. Her shoulders soon loosened up and she was having no trouble keeping up with her share of the paddling. Nic kept them close to the banks, or rather, the edges of the flood.

They were on the river a few hours when it happened. One moment she turned to say something to Nic as they skimmed along on the water and the next she was under it. Instinctively, she clawed and kicked her way toward light and air, fighting the drag of her clothes and boots. She broke the surface to the sound of Nic's frantic shouts.

'Angle across the current to the bank!' His voice came from behind her and she sensed he was in the water, too.

Nic had taught her to swim in the Sonhos and she was a strong swimmer. But the riverbank was moving past at frightening speed, and her hampered efforts at swimming seemed feeble against the power of the current. She dared not stop struggling for a moment to take off her boots or clothes, or to see if Nic still had his head above water.

Gradually she was being carried toward the bank. At last she could reach out toward the roots of trees that had been undercut by the rushing water. She managed to crook her arm around one that she snatched at as she flew by.

The force of the water whipped her

around to face upstream and she grabbed the root with her other arm to secure her hold. Nic was bobbing toward her, his head as much under the water as out of it. He appeared to be fighting the current using only one arm, his right.

She twined both legs around the root and pulled herself free of the sucking water. Then she extended her right hand to him as he was swept toward her. If their outstretched hands failed to clasp . . .

He grabbed her forearm just in time, and she clamped her fingers around his, the way he'd taught her at the rock formation. She held on until he kicked his way out of the raging torrent into a little backwater among the plants on the bank. Meanwhile, her shoulder felt like it was being ripped out of its socket.

Once he was clear, she inched her way backward along the root, dangling above the water, until she was able to drop into the thick green growth beside him. They lay panting, gagging, and retching, side by side.

'Are we normal yet?' he asked plaintively, once he caught his breath.

'Don't, Nic. Are you all right?' she asked around a cough that threatened to choke her.

'I've been better,' he gasped. 'It's really true. Your life *does* flash before your eyes when you're drowning. I think I swallowed half the Sonhos.'

'Then I swallowed the other half.' He was right. The video bytes of her life that had played in her head had been mostly of Nic and a few of her dad, and one very clear one of her mother.

She raised herself on one elbow and looked down at him. A bright red stain colored the water and leaves where Nic lay. She gawked at it a moment, forgetting to breathe. Then she was on her feet, bending over him with her hands hooked under his arms, pulling him farther into the slight indentation they'd made in the vegetation. He pushed with his feet, and her heart leapt into her throat when he moaned softly.

'You're strong, Jungle Eyes, a woman who can hold her own in a fight. I like that.' He ended with a smile, his eyes closed.

He winced when she started to unbutton what was left of his shirt, thought better of it, and simply popped the remaining buttons down the front.

'On second thought,' he added, 'be gentle with me.'

Her breath left her in a hissing rush when she saw the gaping, ragged tear in the fleshy part of his left shoulder.

'Shut up, Nic,' she managed to gasp. 'And stop bleeding, right this minute. What happened out there?' She was aware that she didn't have long to stop the bleeding before he passed out.

'A floating tree, what else? I caught a glimpse of it just before it hit us. I didn't have time to do anything about it. Good thing we were so near the riverbank.'

'And did this tree bite you?' She

scrabbled around in the greenery, looking for big leaves.

'Well, since I was handy and it was having a bad day, too . . . There was a sharp point where a branch had broken off. It caught me as I rolled over the trunk. It went in then tore. How bad — ?' He lifted his head to look at the wound then let it fall back against the vegetation. 'At least my arm is still there. I wasn't sure.'

Watching his blood flow from his flesh, she felt panic welling up inside her. She found some broad leaves from a low plant and applied pressure with them over the wound. He yelped.

'What should I do? Tell me what to do! This shouldn't be happening. We gave it back. Are we supposed to pay interest?' Her voice shot up shrilly and she bit her lip as she dragged the pitch down to within the range of human hearing. 'Everything's gone,' she said raggedly. 'I don't have anything to clean it, to bandage it. You need stitches, antibiotics.'

He touched her arm and immediately she felt calmer. 'Easy, Copper Top. Don't lose it now because I need you. Just do what you're doing and we'll take it from there. We don't have a wide range of choices here.'

When the bleeding slowed, she made a fresh wad of leaves for Nic to hold against his shoulder. He struggled to his knees. She watched him closely as he crouched there for a minute, white and perspiring. When he recovered enough to stand up, she pulled the gleaming machete from its sheath on his belt, preparing to cut through the thick stuff around them into the forest proper.

'Be careful,' he warned. 'Remember I sharpened it again yesterday. Firm grip, swing wide, keep your left arm and legs clear. Just go straight through. It shouldn't be far.'

She put her left arm behind her back and used broad, side to side swinging motions well out in front of her. With chinging sounds, the broad blade sliced its way through anything it came in contact with.

Once through the bank of vegetation along the river's edge, they stood on the rain forest floor among trees that rose a hundred feet and more. The layered green canopy blocked out the morning light and cast the decaying, leafy carpet beneath their feet into perpetual twilight.

Now she looked at the beauty around them with fear. The walking itself wouldn't be too difficult, but with Nic hurt, the distance in any direction to medical help, even an Indian medicine man, was daunting.

She helped him sit down against the buttressed roots of a forest giant, and they took stock of what they had in their pockets. Luiz apparently had put Nic's identification wallet into the pocket of one pair of shorts, the pair he wore now. It held his badge and ID card and a plastic credit card. Besides the wallet, his pockets held a length of heavy, reinforced string, his pocket

knife and switchblade, two handkerchiefs, a few coins, and a butane lighter.

'We can have a fire tonight,' she said
when she saw the lighter.

'Maybe,' he replied grimly, trying it.
'It's old. I meant to replace it.' He
quickly extinguished the reluctant
flame.

Her turned-out pockets brought
forth two handkerchiefs, chewing gum,
the large plastic bottle of aspirin from
last night, still dry, some soggy dried
fruit, and a supply of water-proof
matches in a small plastic vial, which
she habitually carried. Nic grunted
when he saw them.

She sighed. 'Sorry. Everything was in
the raft.' She half rose. 'Maybe I
could — '

He grabbed her hand. 'Stay away
from that river. It's all gone. Don't even
think about trying to find anything
from the raft.'

He glanced down at their pitiful little
pile of resources. She saw him frown.
'I've had more river experience than

you and this is all I can come up with? I know better than to carry everything in a pack. I usually have more useful things in my pockets.'

She felt the need to reassure him and tried to inject confidence into her voice. 'You have knowledge of Indian ways and the rain forest. I have a little specialized knowledge of plants. At least we should be able to find food and water and shelter. But first, we have to tend to your shoulder. I can use palm thorns as needles and palm fibers as sutures.'

'There's another method,' he said slowly. 'I saw some Indians use it once.'

'Oh? Well, I'll take a quick look around for one of those palms. You stay here and rest.' She jumped to her feet.

Again he shook his head and caught her hand as she took a step. 'You know better, Gabby,' he said severely. 'We need each other too much to risk becoming separated, and the ability to walk is a precious commodity to me right now. Let's start moving downstream while there's light. Your palm or my ants, the one we find first is the one we'll use.'

'Ants? Did you say ants?' she asked in disbelief, but he refused to tell her any more.

They walked a couple of hours, with Nic in the lead. She watched him, prepared to help him if he needed her.

Just as she was going to suggest a rest stop, she caught a movement off to her right. A tiny brown bird, whose only beauty was in its acrobatic flight, settled onto a plant that grew alone on the forest floor. Almost immediately it spiraled into the air again and flew off. A tiny bird twisting in flight. *The first figure on the medallion.*

She sucked in her breath while chills rippled up and down her spine. The plant was one her father had shown her and told her never to forget. Without thinking, she quietly veered away from Nic to kneel beside the lanceleaf plantain. That she should find it now, when Nic needed it so desperately, gave her a new round of goose bumps.

In another second, Nic's voice, with a hint of panic in it, rose in a shout as he called her name.

'I'm over here,' she answered, standing up and waving to him excitedly. 'We're stopping right here, right now to clean that gash. I found a plant whose leaves have antiseptic properties. I'll pulp them between two rocks, mix them with water, and clean your shoulder.'

'Don't do that,' he said as he wobbled to a halt beside her.

'Do what? Do you see any small rocks?' She looked around her, pushing aside the low growth with her boots.

'Don't disappear like that. Please. For the sake of my sanity?'

Something in his voice made her look at him. 'Sorry, Nic. I was afraid I wouldn't be able to find the plant again if I didn't stop — '

'That's what I'm afraid of, too, only it's you I'm afraid I'll lose. You know you have to tell me when you're stopping, Gabby.' His face was white and was covered with a sheen of perspiration.

She was immediately filled with remorse. Nic was hurt and it was all her fault.

'You're right, Nic, I do know better. You rest here beside the plant. I'll stay where you can see me while I look for what I need. If I get out of sight, you can shout swear words at me in Portuguese and English and I'll follow the sounds back to their source.' She was rewarded by a feeble grin.

She found two small, flat stones then a stiff-leafed, cup-like bromeliad with rain water in it, growing on a fallen tree. She cleaned the moss off the stones with a little of the water. She pulped the plantain leaves between them, mixing the pulp with the water in the bromeliad. When she had enough, she used their handkerchiefs to clean the gash, inside and out, with the green liquid. Nic held up to the pain better than she did.

'It's burning,' he said through gritted teeth. 'Does that mean it's working?'

'Let's hope so.'

With shaking hands, she repacked the wound with bruised plantain leaves. Before they moved on she cut some flexible liana vine and made a pouch out of a broad leaf. In it she put the stones and the bromeliad with the remaining liquid inside, then she tied the pouch to one of her belt loops. Nic grinned when she lobbed off the whole lanceleaf plantain and tied it, using more liana, around her waist so that it hung down in back like a bustle.

The dim light overhead seemed to be coming straight down on them when Gabby saw Nic look closely at some black ants, over an inch and quarter long, that were scurrying over the exposed roots of a fallen tree. She tried to hurry past but he grabbed her sleeve.

'Please tell me those are the wrong kind of ants,' she begged quietly. 'I'm sure there's a thorny palm just around the next corner.'

Nic leaned against the trunk of the fallen tree and slid down it to a sitting position. 'Sorry. You know as well as I do that most rain forest plants grow miles apart from each other. We could walk for a week before we find that palm.'

He was panting and took a minute to rest before he continued. 'Listen carefully, Gabby, because I don't have enough energy to say this again. You have to pick up one ant at a time, leaving its head and biting jaws free. They also sting, so you'll have to use leaves to pick them up.'

She listened with growing horror as he went on.

'The ant's jaws will be spread, ready to bite. I'll pinch the edges of the wound together and you hold the ant against it. When it clamps its jaws together through the skin, cut off its head with my switchblade. It's a strange but effective suture.'

She moaned and slid down the tree

trunk to land with a plop beside him. Her insides twisted.

A sudden hissing sound overhead filtered through her consciousness. Frightened, she turned her face upward as the first raindrops reached them through the canopy of leaves. The torrential afternoon rain had begun.

'Perfect timing,' she said and felt like shaking her fist toward the skies.

'Isn't it always?' he agreed.

Once she reconciled herself to the grisly task at hand, she set up shop in the tree's exposed roots, which gave them some cover and was close to their source of 'sutures.' She dabbed at the edges of the wound with the 'antiseptic' before putting in the 'sutures.' She dipped each ant headfirst into the mixture, as a precaution.

The ants' strong biting jaws made a sickening popping sound as they broke through Nic's skin. He couldn't hide the pain and a groan escaped once. It took a long time for her to perfect her technique. They took a break so each of them could throw up.

'Stop being so damned brave, Nic. Pretend you're alone and free to express what you're feeling. Groan, scream, curse, howl if you want to. I'm about to myself,' she admitted as they braced themselves to continue.

'Talk to me, Gabby,' he gasped. 'Anything. Just let me hear your voice.'

She did. She told him all about her trials, some of them funny, in setting up a man's business in a macho country. She related the propositions, the pinches, the squeezes, and the outright gropes she endured. And she told him all that changed to respect when they saw how she could fly, when they saw their cargoes arrive in one piece, all at a decent price. She grew tired of the sound of her own voice.

It was a blessing to both of them when he passed out. Tears had dried on her cheeks by the time she finished an hour later. Neat rows of black 'sutures' snaked across his skin like the Indians' tattoos.

She dreaded having to put both of them through the ordeal again should the 'sutures' tear out, so she tied the remains of his shirt into a temporary sling.

Nic drifted in and out. When he started to come around, she half carried, half walked him around and into the opposite end of the huge, hollow trunk of the fallen tree. He lay back, deathly pale and drenched with perspiration, against the spongy, rotted wood.

During the downpour, she set out cups that she fashioned out of rolled up leaves to catch the rain for drinking water. The soiled handkerchiefs went out into the rain, too, on the tree's trunk. She gave him three aspirin with several cups of water.

'How's your hand?' he asked, his voice weak.

One of the ants had managed to sting her before its beheading. The fiery pain had subsided, leaving a dull throb around the swelling.

'They pack quite a punch, at both ends.' She sank down beside him.

He adjusted his position slightly so their shoulders and thighs touched. Gabby found herself leaning against him, some unseen force drawing her.

'I wish we had something more than aspirin for the pain. I'm sorry I hurt you.' She couldn't keep the anguish out of her voice.

'No 'I'm sorries.' But it felt so good when you stopped.' He grinned lopsidedly at her and her heart lurched painfully.

'What should we do now?' she asked after a few minutes.

He took her hand in his free one, a long-fingered, tawny contrast against the slim fairness of hers. 'Since I'm in no condition to manfully throw you over my shoulder Tarzan-style and carry you out of the jungle to safety, why don't we get some firewood while the rain has decided to give us a break. We'll find something to eat, then rest so we can move on at dawn.'

She nodded, sorry that he could only think of her as a friend, or worse yet, a little sister. Although she was certain he hadn't kissed her like either of those.

She had lost count of how many Brazilian men had explained their 'needs' to her followed by their suggestions for her part in satisfying those needs, all of which she declined. And Nic was a healthy, virile man — until she got her hands on him.

One thing she was sure of, whatever she felt for him now was growing stronger every minute she spent with him. For one wild moment, she had wanted to kiss away his pain.

Neither of them had moved yet. 'Will you be able to walk tomorrow?' she asked.

'A little better than you could the other night.' His smile made her feel wobbly, inside and out. 'We have a long walk to the mission hospital at Grilo.'

He turned his face away and she realized that there was something else coming. Something unpleasant.

'We have to be realistic about this, Gabby. Because of the climate I'll develop a raging fever and infection very soon. Don't let me wander away from you. Until you have to, that is. You might have to go on alone. You have to prepare yourself for that.'

She kicked at the rotting wood with one boot. 'Don't even think it, Nic. I got you into this and I will get you out. How far is Grilo?'

He shrugged then winced with pain. 'Our time in the air from the Amaral village to the formation, and from the formation to where we ditched, is a blessing, and we made good time yesterday and this morning on the river at the speed it's running. An easy walk is twenty miles a day. This isn't an easy walk. We'll be lucky to do eight, if you can keep me on my feet and moving.'

Aware he hadn't answered her question, her mind raced, searching for alternatives. 'Shouldn't we go back to the Amarals?'

He slowly shook his head, his eyes

closed. 'Come on, Gabby, think about it. I'd rather put my energy into moving toward a real doctor.

'Besides, I'm not sure they would send a runner to Grilo for me. I had to threaten them with armed intervention from headquarters before they would agree to the 'moon' compromise and meet with the Nunes. Stories about our fathers, red hair, green eyes, and bubbles buy only so much, you know. Paul and medical help are at Grilo, and a radio. And maybe Paul will send out a search party when we don't turn up.'

Her voice was tiny with guilt. 'I'm sorry, Nic. I'll get us out of this somehow. I swear it.'

He turned his head against the wood to look at her. 'No guilt trips, Gabby, please. You're impetuous and enthusiastic. You couldn't have known this would happen.'

This time she struck both her fists against her drawn-up knees as tears of frustration pricked her eyelids.

'Me, too,' he said and reached for

one of her clenched fists. 'Don't waste your energy, Gabby.'

Her fingers relaxed at his touch. He examined the swelling on the heel of her hand then lifted it to his lips and very deliberately pressed his lips against the spot in a warm, lingering kiss that had her gasping softly. Immediately the pain lessened.

'Come on, let's find some wood and our supper,' he said in a throaty whisper, releasing her hand.

11

They decided to shelter for the night in their fallen tree. It supplied twigs, but they had to search farther afield for kindling and larger pieces of wood. She made two trips with armfuls of wood, with Nic carrying what he could. Then they went foraging for food.

He pointed out a small palm in the growth along the river and told her to cut a few fronds to shave to start their fire. After she cut the fronds, she cut off the young palm at its base and took out the crisp, whitish heart. Maybe they could eat it raw, like celery, or roast it over the fire. She used her shirttail as a basket and put the palm heart in it.

She spotted a wild pineapple, a relative of the stiff, spiky, rosette-like bromeliads that clung to almost every tree, living and dead, they'd come across. She cut out the small fruit from the center of the plant and added it to her food basket.

'I guess this is it,' she said when they got back to their tree. She hadn't seen anything else to forage. 'We'd better eat the dried fruit that got wet, before it molds. Do you have anything else in mind?'

He answered her with a question of his own. 'What kind of fisherman are you now?'

He sounded stronger and that gave her heart. 'The same kind I was when we were kids. The reluctant kind. I draw the line at catching them with my bare hands or with my teeth.'

Grinning, he pulled the wire-reinforced string from his pocket and held it up.

She eyed it warily. 'Hmmm. Unless I'm supposed to lasso them, we'll need something to use as a hook.'

His gaze swept the thick vegetation along the river's edge. 'If there's any bamboo growing nearby, we can make a hook out of it. But I don't see any. The

Indians sometimes use curved thorns,'
he added.

She snapped her fingers as an idea
came to her. 'I could make a spear
using your switchblade.'

He frowned and shook his head.
'Only as a last resort, Gabby. The river
is too dangerous for spear fishing.'

She stared at the string, trying to
forget her rumbling stomach. Hunger
must surely be the mother of *some*
invention. She remembered the jagged
points of an expired credit card she had
cut up and thrown away before she left
Sao Paulo.

'Give me the credit card in your
identification wallet,' she said, holding
out her hand. 'I can use one of your
knives to cut some hooks out of it.'

'Don't leave home without it,' he
said, giving her the whole wallet and
both knives.

While she was cutting and shaping
the strong plastic, Nic went to the
opposite end of their fallen tree, the end
where the black ants lived, and struck it

with the machete, exposing a writhing mass of grubs beneath the bark. He brought back a rolled leaf full of them for bait.

She punched a hole with the switchblade in the end of one of the flat, sharp hooks she'd cut out of the plastic. When she poked the string through the hole, Nic helped her securely knot it. They attached the other end of the string to a sturdy piece of wood that she could hold like a bobbin of kite string. He impaled a grub on the hook's point while she held it steady for him.

She cleared a path with the machete to the river. At the water's edge, Nic sat down on some leaves to watch, his eyes never stopping as they scanned the water around them for danger. While she waited for a tug on the line, she felt the corners of her mouth lift.

'Why are you smiling?' he asked after a minute.

She chuckled in answer. 'This reminds me of one of those old recipes that begin with 'First you catch and kill your — ' '

Something had taken the hook so fiercely that it almost tipped her forward into the water. Just how strong was Nic's reinforced string, she wondered? She certainly couldn't wind it up with whatever was on the end of the line pulling it so taut. Nic was struggling to rise from his perch to help her, when she simply turned and ran up the narrow trail they had made, pulling a fat, oval black fish clear of the water as she did so.

Nic tried to behead it with the machete. It bit down so hard on the blade that its teeth snapped off and scattered like a broken string of pearls. He put his boot on it and held it down.

'Is that what I think it is?' She was staring at the remaining bristling, thorn-like teeth that seemed to fill its head, which now lay some distance away from its body.

'Piranha,' Nic said simply. 'The flesh is sweet and good.'

'It looks to be more mouth than meat,' she observed, keeping her distance. 'I'm glad he and his buddies didn't notice us in the water.'

They managed to catch nine more within as many minutes, using the same technique, before Nic called a halt. She cleaned the fish near the water, under his guidance, and laid the filets on a broad leaf to carry back to the tree.

They built their fire at the grub-and-ant end of the section of hollow tree, which she hoped would send the ants scurrying elsewhere. Soon some of the fish and the palm heart were spitted over the fire, with the rest of the fish cut into slivers to cure in the smoke.

They took off their boots and socks and put them near the flames to dry out. Gabby took great pains to build a rack out of some of their kindling. She spread the remaining lanceleaf plantain leaves on it to dry so she could carry them unspoiled with her on their journey.

When the food was ready, they ate

their fill of the fish, divided the vegetable, pineapple, and dried fruit, and drank fresh rain water.

Feeling much better on a full stomach, Gabby held up one of the conical cups she had made out of broad leaves and set out in the rain. 'To our survival skills, Nic.'

'I hope they're good enough,' he responded.

She noticed that his head was nodding and his eyelids looked heavy. 'Come on, let's go to our end of the 'house' and get some rest. I'll sit up, so I can keep the fire going.'

Before they left the fire, she cleaned his wound, using the last of the first batch of antiseptic. The shoulder didn't look as bad as she was afraid it might. At least she felt no heat of fever while she worked. She gave him more aspirin.

'May I borrow your shoulder for a while, Gabby?' he asked when they were settled inside the spongy wooden tunnel of rotted out tree trunk.

'Anything to make you as comfortable as possible, Nic. You can stretch out and use me for a pillow, if you like.'

Again at his touch, a sense of calmness descended upon her, relaxing her whole body. He was asleep almost immediately. She cautiously looked around the walls of their temporary shelter, dimly lit by the fire at the other end. In life its girth had been so great that in death its rotted shell was almost high enough for her to stand upright in. It was dry and nothing was moving, so she leaned her head against the soft cushion of Nic's thick hair and closed her eyes.

Thunder woke her a few hours later. She eased away from Nic and went to the other end to add wood to the fire and to check on their boots and socks, the smoked fish, and the precious leaves. Nic hadn't moved when she returned, so she inched up to him, put her head on his good shoulder, and fell asleep.

She awoke to a stiff neck and Nic's hot gaze directed upward at her. He had stretched out sometime in the night and used her lap for a pillow. His cheeks were slightly flushed and his breathing was fast and shallow. His beard had grown overnight, making him look like a pirate. A feverish pirate.

When she was fully awake, he spoke. 'I have to ask you something, Gabby. Remember those walls I built when I came back to Brazil? The ones I told you about?'

For a moment she wondered if he was delirious already. Then she remembered what he'd said when he told her about Nicky.

'The thick and high and cold ones?' she repeated from memory.

He maneuvered around so that his head rested near her knees and he could look up into her face at a more comfortable angle. 'The very ones. How did you get past them so quickly?'

She rubbed the back of her neck and smiled down at him. 'You know me,

Nic. I just ran into them, like I did with The Duck into your dock, and they fell right down.'

He smiled back at her, his teeth white against his tanned face and dark stubble.

She pressed her palm against his forehead, then followed it with her cheek, something she remembered her mother doing. 'Oh, God, you do have a fever,' she said, dreading the words and the sense of panic that came with them. 'I'll get you some more aspirin and water.'

In an instant he grasped her loose top knot of hair with his good hand and pulled her head down until his mouth could claim hers. Abandoning herself to the delight of his kiss, she cradled his head and echoed the movement of his lips, hot with fever, across the coolness of hers.

Finally, she broke away from him. 'What's happening here, Nic? To us?' she asked him breathlessly.

'This friendship of ours is catching

fire, Gabby,' he whispered. 'Haven't you noticed?'

'Oh, *I've* noticed.' She gently stroked his rough cheek. 'But I wasn't sure it was happening for you, that maybe it was just because I was *here*, alone with you.'

He shook his head. 'I was falling hard that last season when I was sixteen. I realized when I kissed you again that nothing has changed.'

Her hand moved to smooth his hair. 'Bad timing, huh? Right in the middle of this mess I catapulted us into.'

His voice was a husky rasp. 'At least we're together again. I wish we had more time, and that I was in better condition to explore this, but there are more pressing matters to think about right now. Like getting our sorry selves to Grilo.'

She smiled down at him. 'Paul told me this should happen between us, but at the time I couldn't imagine it. Now I can't imagine us apart. But for the moment you'll have to get off me so I can get you some aspirin and water.'

They ate most of the smoked fish, then she made up a new solution of antiseptic and cleaned his shoulder. It was pink and slightly swollen. She swallowed her fear for him, guilt giving it a bitter taste.

'Be on the lookout for big, strong, broad-leafed plants today, Nic. I can make a sling for you out of them so you can wear your shirt.' She put the remaining dried leaves into her leaf pouch.

They drank their fill from the leaf cups she had left out in the rain all night, but there was no way to carry water with them. Maybe later she would find something from the gourd family that she could hollow out and use as a canteen.

When it was time to leave, Nic struggled to his feet, swaying. Gabby supported some of his weight until he was steady enough to walk.

She looked back at their fallen tree as they moved off. 'It wasn't much, but it was beginning to feel like home,' she told him.

His voice was strained with the effort of walking. 'Nothing but the best accommodations for the Nic and Gabby Road Show.'

After a few minutes, Nic rallied and took the lead, keeping up a steady pace through the morning with only a couple of stops. Her hunger had her seriously looking for food well before mid-day. It would have to be something that didn't require cooking. They had agreed to one fire, at night.

A series of booming roars broke out in a treetop, interrupting her food fantasy. When she looked up, a howler monkey looked back at her.

Nic said in a matter-of-fact voice, 'Bananas.'

She thought he was fantasizing about food. 'You can do better than that, surely, although I'd settle for them right now. I'd imagine a steak. And what I wouldn't give for a cup of coffee.'

He pointed. 'Ba-nan-as,' he repeated carefully.

Then she saw the short tree with a cascade of familiar fruit growing some distance away, right below the howler's perch. She looked from the howler to the bananas and back again. The sturdy, full-throated howler monkey stared solemnly back at her. Howlers usually travel in groups. Yet here was a lone howler calling their attention to . . .

' . . . bananas,' she echoed thoughtfully.

'And you *seem* so intelligent most of the time,' Nic told her dryly.

'Shut up, Nic.' She took the machete from him and approached the tree.

'Don't touch it,' he warned. 'Just lob it off, let it fall, and see if anything crawls out.'

She cut off the stalk of neatly spaced fruit, stepped back when it dropped, flipped it over with one booted foot, and jiggled it with the machete before she picked it up by the stalk end and dragged it to where he sat on the ground. When Nic turned away for a moment, she cut off a big bunch and tossed them toward the now-silent howler's tree.

'They're untouched,' Nic commented. 'It's lucky we got to them before he did. It would have been so easy to miss them.'

Gabby threw the howler an uneasy glance. *The second figure on the medallion.* 'Lucky,' she repeated.

Nic ate two bananas and, using restraint, she ate four of the short, fat, green fruit. They weren't as sweet as the yellow variety she'd brought upriver with her, but they were filling and would keep well. She divided the remaining smoked fish from breakfast between them. They needed to find drinking water now, to replace what they'd lost through perspiration. She wanted to give Nic more aspirin, too, while he had food on his stomach.

She wondered if he connected the monkey with the medallion. The bananas had been pointed out to *him*, although she would have noticed. A howler in full voice is hard to ignore. She doubted he'd seen the tiny bird that brought the lanceleaf plantain to *her* attention. That left — the jaguar. What might a jaguar portend? Probably a menu and they'd be on it.

She spotted some bromeliads growing on a fallen tree that was hung up against another. Nic protested when he saw what she was about to do.

She avoided his grasp when he reached out to stop her. 'We need water, Nic. I'll be careful.'

He handed her the machete. She crawled part way up the trunk then straddled it, bouncing to see how firmly the fallen tree was wedged against its still-growing fellow. Then she inched her way up to where the bromeliads were within reach. She was aware of Nic's watchful eyes as he waited below.

'There's some protein in there, too, compliments of a mother tree frog.' She handed him the first of the 'cups' and three aspirins. 'I can't strain out all the tadpoles with my fingers.'

She made many trips up the slanted trunk, slicing off the stiff upper leaves of the spiky bromeliads and backing down the trunk far enough to hand him their cup-like bases. She drank hers astride the tree.

After her last trip, she cut some of the leaves off the banana tree and a few of the small, flexible liana vines that had climbed from the forest floor to the tree branches high above.

When she had everything she needed, she made up the green solution in some rain water she found in a depression in a stone. She cleaned the hot, swollen wound then soaked one of the handkerchiefs in the liquid and laid it over the gash before covering it.

She made a banana-leaf sling for him and tied it behind his neck and around his body with the liana vines. Then she shook out his shirt and helped him into it, leaving it open to accommodate the sling.

He watched, fascinated, as she tied the remaining bananas, one by one, on two twisted lengths of the leftover liana vine. She wrapped the rope of bananas around her waist twice and tied the ends.

She stood up finally, holding out a hand to him. 'Ready to move on?'

She saw him shake his head as he looked at her banana belt, then he grasped her hand so she could help him to his feet.

12

By late afternoon, with increasingly frequent stops, Nic was exhausted, and she wasn't far behind.

'Here's a tree with buttressed roots,' she said when she saw him stumble. 'We can spend the night between them and catch some more fish to cook.'

'I'm not hungry. Let's find some water.'

The forest floor was overgrown in this area, making walking difficult. There were many liana vines, some as thick as Nic's forearms. The bigger ones were covered with bark, like miniature trees. They reminded Gabby of bars, and moving through them was almost like tackling an obstacle course. She didn't see any fallen trees or bromeliads, though.

Nic looked at the vines closely. 'There's one kind of liana that holds water,' he explained. 'The Indians use it when they're out hunting. Here are a few.' He indicated several lianas that grew close together and looked a little different from their neighbors. 'You'll have to cut a piece eighteen feet long to get one pint, though.'

She studied the liana so she would recognize it next time. 'I'll cut this one off at ground level and you get ready to drink. If I climb one of these big vines near it, I can cut the water liana from above. It should drain by gravity if I hold on to it up there.'

Water trickled out when she made her first cut. It ran in a steady stream when she made the second cut twelve feet up. She let Nic drink his fill then came down and made some leaf cups. They looked for more of the water lianas. She managed to fill some leaf cups by using flexible vines to tie the water lianas in place above before she cut them. She then climbed down and cut the vine at ground level while Nic handed her the cups to fill.

Thunder was rumbling overhead when she approached the tall, solid, buttressed roots of the tree. It smelled strongly of wild boar, but as long as the occupant wasn't home ... With a branch, she thoroughly swept out the four-foot space between two of the roots then settled Nic inside where he could see her.

Her body ached from climbing and walking all day. Her shoulder still bothered her, too, from the awful wrenching it took while she was helping Nic out of the river.

Machete in hand, she searched the immediate area for broad-leafed plants to make a roof over their rough shelter. She was able to reach the solid, fan-shaped leaves of a short palm tree. She dragged the palm fronds back to their tree and arranged them across the four-foot high buttresses.

She made a second shelter in between the adjacent set of roots, for their fire. By then Nic was recovered enough to help her catch and clean the fish for their supper. Again they put their boots and socks near the fire to dry and smoked some extra fish for the next day. Gabby was numb with fatigue by the time they finished eating. She had to force Nic to eat.

She was giving him his aspirin just as the first raindrops fell. They left their fire and moved into the sleeping shelter. She took her flat stones out of her leaf pouch and pulverized some of the dried plantain leaves into one of the leaf cups of water. The other cups were outside, refilling in the rain.

Nic's fever soared as night was falling. He was almost asleep by the time she finished mixing the antiseptic. Losing the light, she hurried. He moaned softly when she pulled back his shirt and untied the liana vines that supported his banana leaf sling. She worked carefully so that both the vines and the leaf could be used again.

She gasped when she saw the hot, swollen, oozing wound. The heat of his fever rose from his skin to warm their shelter. Wringing out the clean hand-kerchief she had hung out in the rain, she dipped it into the solution and cleaned the area. The soiled, smelly handkerchief and the one that had been against his skin all day she then put outside, over the root in the rain. Again she used a clean handkerchief soaked with solution over the wound. By the time she finished he was awake.

She tried not to meet his eyes in the fading natural light, barely enhanced by the fire next door. She was more frightened for him than she could let him know. Gangrene was a very real possibility, and she could feel herself weakening after one day of walking and foraging. How long could she take care of him? For the first time she considered the possibility that they wouldn't survive this brutal trek.

She forced desperate brightness into her voice. 'I'll change the dressing a couple of times tonight. I made enough solution to last until morning.'

He was drifting away again and his

words were slurred. 'Promise me, Gabby, that if both of us get out of this, you'll come back to play with me in the rain forest again, only not like when we were kids. How about Jane to my Tarzan? I see endless possibilities in this situation, if I didn't feel so lousy.'

She smiled into the thickening darkness, a tribute to his spirit. 'It's a promise, Nic. We'll talk about it more after we get out of this mess that I got us into. And thanks for not saying 'I told you so.' '

His voice was a whisper now. 'I decided we would take our chances on the river the second day. My fault for trying to make good time. Save yourself, Gabby. I won't make it to Grilo — '

'Don't say that, Nic,' she interrupted fiercely. 'Don't even think it because it's not an option. We go on or we don't, but we'll do it together. If you want me to live then you have to fight to live, too. Because I swear, Nic, they'll find our bones intermingled where we fall, an idiot hanging on to her last victim.'

There was just enough light for her to see him smile before he fell asleep.

In the wee hours of the morning, he awoke with a chill, his teeth chattering. 'Gabby? Where are we?'

'We're in the forest.' She cradled his head. 'Here, sip some water. We're on our way to the mission hospital at Grilo.'

Tears of fear and helplessness teased her eyelids. She admitted to herself that if he died and she lived, her future would yawn before her like a black chasm, because she loved him, and she had never loved before.

She felt him shake his head in the darkness. 'Not travelling fast enough. So cold.'

She sighed and got to her knees in the cramped space to change his dressing, mostly by touch. He was shuddering violently by the time she finished.

'C-Cold, G-Gabby. W-Warm me.'

All she had left to give him was her

body heat. She made him turn onto his right side, then she took off her shirt and snuggled up against his back, covering them with the double layer of their tattered shirts. Heat from his body burned through her bra and shorts. She wrapped her left arm around him and held him close to her. He was sleeping deeply, more quietly now, long before she closed her eyes again.

It was dawn when the sound woke her, the deep-throated, coughing growl of a big cat. She wasn't too surprised. She edged out from under their shirts and away from Nic's back, reaching for the machete that leaned against one of the buttressed roots. Nic stirred as she drew a shaky breath then cautiously crawled out of their shelter.

She didn't see the jaguar at first, merged into the forest's dappled early morning light. The golden centers inside the black markings on its tawny coat blended into the background, a hidden picture within a picture, until it moved, lifting its nose and winding the smoked fish scent in the air.

She gaped at it, her mouth falling open in silent awe. The animal the Indians call the spirit of the rain forest, the most elusive animal living in it, the one creature her father and Nic's father had never seen in their many travels, stood twenty-five feet away from her in all its glory.

Then its golden eyes fixed themselves on her, their message clear: Nothing personal, you understand, it's just what I do, they told her.

She raised the machete in front of her and slid her gaze away from its stare, a challenge in the animal world. 'You can have the fish, if you're hungry.' She addressed the bush beside it in a clear, quiet voice. 'But to get to him, you have to go through me.'

The jaguar tensed at the sound of her voice. When she stopped speaking, it emitted a huffing rumble.

'That's the deal,' she continued. 'If you don't like it then b-bring it on, Sunshine.' She adjusted her stance and took a firmer grip on the machete's wood handle. Behind her she heard the click and hiss of Nic's switchblade.

The jaguar took one step back then froze, its eyes fixed on something to her right, the way they'd come last night. Gabby turned her head slightly in that direction, taking her gaze off the big cat at the last second.

A huge battle-scarred wild boar stood winding scent twenty feet away, his sharp, curving yellow tusks raised, his tiny piggy eyes squinting nearsightedly. This was no ordinary peccary. Somewhere in this guy's background was an escapee from a farm who had mingled with the local ladies, resulting in this, the military model of a peccary. She blinked when, with a grunt, the boar whirled and trotted away into the undergrowth. The jaguar, long and lithe, leaped after it, melting into the shadows in majestic silence.

'Let's get out of here, Gabby. It's getting crowded,' Nic whispered, retracting his blade and sliding the knife into his pocket.

Gabby stared after the animals, speaking in a dazed voice. 'I've never seen a wild boar that size. With tusks that long and sharp. And we were in his lair. We could have stumbled right into him or he could have attacked us in there.'

'Nasty customer. Thanks to the jaguar, we avoided both scenarios.'

'Yes, thanks to the jaguar,' she repeated in a toneless voice. The jaguar. *The third figure on the medallion.* And they hadn't been on his menu.

Nic's voice grew stronger. 'I don't believe it. You took on a jaguar before breakfast. And in your underwear to boot.'

'He started it. Maybe he heard about your hatband,' she said, turning to him.

He was holding out her shirt to her with one finger. She saw him swallow as his eyes slid over her lacy bra and the pronounced, generous mounds of her breasts beneath it. She took the shirt and handed him the machete to hold while she shrugged it on.

She was suddenly self-conscious. She and Nic had gone swimming together buck naked when they were children. Now, his look brought back that humming awareness that was new to her. She hastily buttoned the shirt and tied the tail in a knot in front.

Feeling warmth in her cheeks, she asked, 'How do you feel?'

He passed a hand across his forehead. 'Like the Anvil Chorus is playing inside my head. Weak. Last night was pretty bad, wasn't it?'

She nodded. 'You settled down after I covered you with our shirts and . . . ' her voice trailed away under his warm look.

'Thanks for the body heat, Gabby. But if I'm delirious, maybe you should keep your distance. I might hurt you.'

She shook her head. 'You weren't combative. You just wanted to get warm. Now, first aid then food and aspirin.'

His fever remained but was lower

during the daylight hours. The food he ate seemed to make a difference.

She foraged as they went, finding avocado pears growing wild. She stuffed their pockets with the fruit before they moved on. The bananas around her waist were good keepers. She would ration them out to herself, she decided, but Nic could have as many as he wanted.

When they shared their smoked fish at noon, using a flat rock for a table, they ate the avocados with it. There were lianas in the area but none were the water lianas they needed so badly. Nic choked down some aspirin with bites of the fruit and they both went thirsty.

They had scarcely finished eating when she sensed frenzied movement on the forest floor. At the same time she felt Nic's body tense and heard his quick intake of breath. Turning, she saw a host of insects jumping, crawling, and flying toward them. Above them flew birds of all shapes and sizes, dipping, chirping, and snatching up the bounty. Frantically, Nic looked around them.

'What is it?' She was suddenly frightened.

His first words came like shots from a gun, hard and fast. 'Army ants. Right now. We have to get out of here. We can try to outrun them but we could meet a splinter group whichever way we go. It's either that or the river.' He looked at her and she could see her own fear reflected in his eyes. There were piranha and caiman in the river.

'Up. Up,' she said, looking around them.

She dismissed the trees with one glance. Nic couldn't climb and there was no handy fallen tree hung up against another that he could crawl up. Her eyes stopped on the group of lianas and she pulled the machete from its sheath, which she now wore on her belt.

With efficient motions, she cut off lengths of thin, flexible, strong liana. She made Nic test one of the thick vines with his weight, then she cut it off at ground level. She pulled the vine over to the boulder that had served as their table, a yard-high, moss-covered flat rock that jutted out of the earth. At the rock's height she cut deep notches into the liana's bark. She tied a big loop in each end of one of the thin liana strips then tied it in strong knots around the bigger vine, inside the notches.

She gave Nic instructions as she worked. 'Climb up on the rock. I'll help you put your feet in the loops. Hang on to the vine with your good arm. I'll cut off more of the vine below your feet when you're aboard.'

There was a high-pitched, ominous buzz in the air and already she could see rust-colored ant scouts scurrying around her boots. She slapped at one that was biting her viciously on the leg. With Nic securely in place, she let the vine swing out over the forest floor, away from the rock. When she cut it off below his vine stirrups, he was safely suspended three feet above the coming danger.

'Move it, Gabby, I see the main column,' Nic prodded.

She tested a nearby liana for herself, as close to Nic's as she could get. She sliced it off at ground level, then chopped a section out of every vine within a five-foot circle around them. There wasn't time to make loops to stand in, so she climbed her vine then reached down and lobbed it off just below her boots.

She wrapped her legs around the vine and locked her feet together, one boot over the other. She couldn't put the machete in its sheath, so she worked the leather thong on its handle over her wrist and let it dangle there.

'Like I've always said, Gabby, poetry in motion.' There was admiration in Nic's weak voice.

She glanced at him. His eyes were closed and his forehead rested against the vine. Could he hold on until the danger passed? If he couldn't and fell . . .

'Just hang on, Nic,' she begged, desperation and fear in her voice. 'If you can't, tell me. I'm close enough to swing over and help you.'

Now the sound was a million miniature buzz saws. Three eight-foot-wide waves of brownish-red ants flowed over everything in sight, spreading out into thinner columns like the fingers of a death-dealing hand. The frantic insects that were trying to escape but weren't fast enough were enveloped and eaten. Every green leaf and stem in sight was devoured.

It was fascinating to watch, for a while, then Gabby turned her attention upward, away from the destruction taking place a yard below where she dangled. The ants had climbed the lianas still growing out of the ground to a height of a yard or more.

A hysterical laugh escaped her before she could stop it. 'High water, *candiru*, a jaguar, army ants. This trip is turning into the plagues of Egypt. Did you see this stuff when you were out here with your dad, or am I a privileged spectator?'

He opened his eyes and looked at her, sending her that crooked grin that was now miraculously connected directly to her heart strings. 'I never saw a jaguar before today. I heard about army ants, but I never saw them in action. Dad did, and he told me about them and what to watch out for.'

'Bless him,' she said softly.

'He said these ants have no permanent home. At night they make a shelter with their bodies, joining legs to form living walls to protect their eggs and their young. Once in a great while, the groups start to move, joining other groups and creating a wave of destruction. Maybe it's the high water that caused them to move. You saved our lives, *querida*.'

A flush of warmth coursed through her when she heard the Portuguese word for 'darling' on his lips.

She kept him talking but it still felt like hours that they hung there, waiting for the columns to pass beneath them. Gabby checked her watch and only half an hour had passed until they were able to climb down. She gave Nic a short time to recover, then hurried him away, to where there were living things and the forest was green.

Nic didn't mention the jaguar again. She hoped its appearance meant the curse was ended, that the interest on the debt was paid in full and fate would allow them to live . . . together. She believed there would be a sign telling her so. She couldn't guess what it would be or when it would happen. She did know that in time she would put all the pieces together and present them to Nic. The facts would be difficult to deny, even for him.

13

Nic wanted to look for shelter early in the afternoon. Their head-on encounters with the rain forest that day brought fatigue early, especially for him. Instead, she pushed him until he staggered and she had to help him.

They entered a rocky area where boulders stood above the low green growth on the forest floor like dark mushrooms. Gabby found a rock ledge with an overhang near a small stream that tumbled over itself on the way to the river. They could hear rapids on the Sonhos above the sound of the stream's rushing.

Nic thought it was safe to drink the water from the stream, but he wouldn't let her near it when she mentioned a bath. Although he was swaying on his feet, he made her choose the place where she would bathe then he checked for *candiru* in the water. A shudder ran through her at the memory.

Before washing up and resting, she gathered wood, built a fire at the edge of their rock shelter, caught fish and cleaned them, spitted them over the flames, made up a batch of solution and cleaned Nic's wound. Only then did she go upstream to get herself as clean as she could without soap.

Too late she discovered that the place she had chosen and he had checked out was within sight of their shelter. She glanced at him and his eyes were closed. Too tired and too dirty to be modest, she climbed down the shallow bank, turned her back to him, and took off her clothes.

She rinsed out her underthings, but she was afraid to wet her shirt or shorts. She might need the shirt to cover Nic later, and she had nothing to wear in the meantime. As it was, both were damp with the afternoon rain.

Nic was still asleep when she carried her underwear back to the fire and hung them up to dry, looking speculatively at her bra. She wondered vaguely if she could turn it into a slingshot. Maybe she could get a monkey or another small animal to make a strengthening broth for Nic. She imagined his face if she suggested it.

She jumped and sucked in her breath when Nic's voice interrupted her musings. Her eyes flew to his face.

His were open and full of mischief. 'Great legs, Gabby. You always had great legs. You've added to the inventory since we used to go skinny dipping in the Sonhos,' he added, winking at her.

Her face flamed. 'You watched me?'

He closed his eyes again and sighed heavily. 'I'm sick, Gabby, not dead.'

'You're a sick *pig*, Nic,' she shot back and was rewarded with a full-blown smile.

Nic threw up the fish she made him eat but later he managed to keep down a few bites of banana and his aspirin. In the blackness of that night, he didn't get chills and she didn't need to keep him warm. He just quietly burned all by himself. The waves of heat that emanated from his body kept the cool rock shelter warm for her.

He did surprisingly well the next day, despite the fact that he could force down only one bite of banana and his aspirin. Again, his fever went down during the daylight hours, but he was very weak and getting weaker.

She walked in the lead or they walked side by side. She kept close watch on him, afraid he would veer away, losing himself in the forest on purpose, so that she would have to go on alone. She would disabuse him of *that* notion when the time was right.

He was able to keep up the sedate pace she set if they made frequent rest stops. She started looking for shelter early in the afternoon. With a mixture of fear and dread, she admitted to herself that Nic had reached the point where he couldn't be pushed anymore today — and probably not tomorrow.

Those were her thoughts as she plodded along with her head down, frantic with worry for Nic, wondering what to do next. Every other step was a fervent prayer for help. She glanced up when she sensed that something stood in their way.

A fallen tree blocked their immediate path. But just beyond it was a wooden trough held up by an efficient network of cross supports. The accompanying roar told her that water rushed down the trough on top. She glanced to the right and the contraption rolled away at a slight incline to disappear into the forest. To their left it continued right through the thick growth at the river's edge, dumping the water into the river itself. The whole thing looked like a miniature wild water ride at an amusement park.

There was a shack in the distance, on the other side of the man-made wooden barrier, and a man was coming out onto its little porch. She was dumbfounded. Nic plowed into her where she stood gaping.

'Oh, Nic, thank God,' she whispered. 'People!' Her arm rose to wave and she felt a cry of greeting rise in her throat.

'No, Gabby!' Nic hissed in her ear.

The next thing she saw was the thick layer of wet leaves that her face was shoved into on the forest floor. A heavy weight was holding her there. Nic had pushed her to the ground beneath him.

'An illegal mining operation,' he whispered harshly against her ear before he rolled to the side and they untangled themselves. 'That's the guard shack. They'll shoot us on sight. Or rather, they'll shoot me, especially in this uniform. You would be the entertainment until they got tired of you.'

Spitting out a leaf, she glanced at the colorful patches on the upper sleeves of the tattered remains of his shirt. Then something in her memory clicked. 'The muddy water running into the Sonhos?' she asked.

He nodded, settling onto his back

and holding his shoulder.

Curious, she raised herself cautiously and peeped over the top of the log. 'He didn't see us. What are they mining?'

He struggled to his knees to join her. 'Gold, probably. That's a sluice. They diverted a stream. We'll have to cut inland to circle around them.'

'I didn't know there was gold up here.' For just a moment excitement overcame all her other emotions.

He snorted. 'Why do you think Dad dragged me upriver every chance he got? This area is on an ancient rock shield. It contains rich, untapped mineral deposits and small deposits of gold and other precious metals. It's just difficult to get to. The upper Sonhos is cut off by those twenty sets of rapids and waterfalls I told you about. There are twelve thousand square miles of endless forest up here. Small, illegal operators can slip in where they like, usually undetected, when they find a vein. This must be a rich find to rate such a sophisticated operation.'

She shifted closer to Nic so she could peer through the camouflaging leaves of a low-growing bush on the other side of the tree trunk. She studied the shack and the man smoking on the small porch. There was something familiar about him, even at this distance. He was big without being fat, and he was wearing his boots unlaced. It hit her like a thunderbolt. She knew Nic would not be amused.

She gave a nervous little laugh. 'Well, what do you know. My old pal Felippe.'

'You know him?' he asked sharply, incredulously.

She looked at him and nodded glumly. 'He's one of Prospero's men. Nasty, and stupid with it. Doesn't understand 'no' from a woman holding a gun.'

Nic was quick. 'And did you use it?'

She felt a slow smile begin. There hadn't been nearly enough of those to suit her since they returned the medallion.

'Well, just to make my point, I put a

round between his boots. I told him the next one would be not quite three feet higher. You taught me to shoot, Nic. I wouldn't have missed. After my demonstration, he figured it out, and he spread the word.'

'Let's get going,' he urged, grinning. 'Who knows how far inland we'll have to go to avoid them.'

She put out a hand to stop him. It came to rest on his forearm. 'Give me another minute. I want to think about this. There has to be a dugout or a boat somewhere around here with our names on it. Maybe there's a river landing near the shack that we can't see from here.' She frowned in concentration. 'We're below most of the rapids now. How do they bring in supplies up here?'

'If this is Prospero's setup then I'd guess from the north, probably by air. He has contacts and operations up there. Remember all that air traffic over my head a few months ago? That's when they set up shop, from one of

Prospero's staging areas by way of Manaus. For now, let's just get around them.'

She wouldn't push the boat stealing idea at that moment. But she was reluctant to leave the river, their directional touchstone, to skirt the edges of this operation. There were probably more guards inland where the action was and they might blunder into one. Besides, Nic couldn't go much farther. Every step they took inland would waste time and Nic's precious energy.

She bit her lower lip as she watched the guard stand up and stretch then walk down the shack's steps. 'Look, he's taking that trail into the forest. I don't see anybody around except him. Let's just stay low and cross here.'

He wiped at the fever sheen on his forehead and she saw reluctant acceptance in his eyes when he realized it was climbing again. Necessity forced them to attempt to cross here.

She stayed at Nic's side, urging him.

The distance was farther than she had anticipated, so she could imagine how it felt to him. He barely made it to the rocks a short distance into the forest on the other side of the shack's clearing. They collapsed in a heap behind the biggest boulder.

There had been no shouts and no shots, but she immediately raised herself to peer over the top of the rock toward the back of the shack and the surrounding area. The guard reappeared out of the forest, heading for the shack.

Nic was gasping for breath. 'Gee, Gabby, you bring me to the nicest places.'

'Be quiet,' she whispered. 'He's coming back to the shack and we're not far enough away from it yet.'

She sent a swift prayer of thanks skyward for what lay before them. She had been right. There was a small cove on a wide, deep stretch of river across from the shack, with lots of tree cover that hid it from the air. A portable dock lay on the beach close to the rising water, and big drums of aviation fuel stood in lines on the sand. There were dugouts, tobacco-colored with age, with motors and paddles in them. She could have wept with relief.

'And you know the most interesting people,' Nic continued wildly in a harsh whisper.

'Hush, Nic!' She implored, looking down at him, his eyes fever-bright in his flushed face. 'It's all right, *querido*, he didn't see us,' she explained softly, brushing his black hair off his burning forehead.

He caught her hand and held it to his lips, pressing their heat against her palm. 'I don't want to die, Gabby. Not now,' he said raggedly. 'I want to make love to you for the rest of our lives and give you those babies you want. I want them to be mine.'

She took his face between her hands, knowing that was exactly what she wanted, too. 'Listen up, Nic,' she said firmly, looking straight into his gray-blue eyes. 'I want them to be yours, too. But if you die on me out here, so help me I'll hold seances and pester you. I won't give you a moment's peace in the hereafter,' she threatened in a fierce whisper.

He gave her that lopsided grin and her heart did flip-flops in her chest. 'You would, too. That's powerful incentive to stay alive,' he agreed.

The next words came from her innermost, private self. She felt her face grow warm. 'There's something else, Nic, something I've never shared with anyone. Me. I'm still a virgin.'

His eyes widened and his lips parted in surprise. 'You've never made love with a man, Gabby?'

She shook her head, holding his eyes with hers. 'Only around the edges. Never all the way, although I came close once.'

'What stopped you?' Interest was apparently getting past the fever.

She had wondered that herself for years. Now, she understood, when it was Nic asking the question. 'He wasn't you, Nic. I realized in this moment that I've been waiting for you, since you kissed me when I was fifteen. You've taught me everything else. I want you to teach me how to make love.'

'Oh, *Deus*,' he moaned, 'and I can barely walk.'

She laughed. Then, as softly as the misty rain that began to fall on them, she briefly touched her lips to his. A spark seemed to leap across the small space between them when she drew back. This time she kissed him soundly, coaxing him to join her in the adrenaline high that was chattering through her system. He obliged.

'Thanks, I needed that,' he whispered as she got to her feet in a crouch to lead him away from the area.

Daylight was waning by the time they found shelter between the buttresses of a tree. She hurriedly fixed a roof for them and made some leaf cups to set out to catch the night's rain. She used the first one to make up the solution to clean his shoulder, setting it aside for the moment.

She was afraid to make a fire, so she ate the bananas she had crushed on her banana belt when Nic pushed her down. He ate two small bites and drank two cups of water with his aspirin.

'So Manoel Prospero is involved in this operation.' Nic was watching her face closely in the failing light and she was very much aware of it. 'Do you know anything about it?'

She moved uneasily in the deepening gloom, meeting his eyes briefly. 'I believe I do, indirectly. I have a lot to tell you, Nic. Brace yourself.'

'Oh, Gabby,' he said, resignation, dismay, and anger flavoring the two words.

She started her evening routine of cleaning the hot, red gash in his shoulder, fearing she would lose the light. It was so swollen now that the 'stitches,' which they had put in at such great cost to both of them, had pulled out. If the heat emanating from his skin was any guide, she was amazed he was still lucid.

'Just hear me out, Nic,' she pleaded, 'because it's a long story. Remember I told you that Prospero held a huge IOU from my dad? He held it for two years, until he needed another pilot. Don't ask me what happened to the one I replaced because I don't know.

'Anyway, when I couldn't pay all of the IOU off with the insurance money I had left, I agreed to work it off by flying for him. I had one condition, though. My cargoes had to be clean, no contraband. He agreed.'

At Nic's disbelieving snort, she stopped and glared at him. 'See, you're making pig noises already. Do you want to hear this or not?'

'I'm hanging on your every word. This is the first fairy tale I've heard in years. How could you be so gullible?' Exasperation lay heavy on the words.

'Thank you *so* much for making this easy for me, Nic,' she replied sweetly. 'Oh, gee, let me think. What could I offer the local bad boy except my livelihood? Oh, I know. My body or my planes! Why didn't I think of that? Would you have preferred that I offer him my body, Nic, because I sure as hell wasn't going to sign over either of my planes!'

He sat upright from his leaning position against one of the buttresses. 'Very funny, Gabrielle. Your father should have beat you when he had the chance.' On a worried note, he added, 'Prospero didn't — '

'No, he didn't suggest it and neither did I, but does that help you see the position I was in? It was a lot of money I owed, Nic, and with the deal he offered I didn't even have to use my own planes.'

When he relaxed again, which she took to mean he understood, she continued. 'You think I'm crazy for trusting him. I don't know how to explain this to avoid pig noises, but we had a sort of grudging respect for each other. I liked him and he liked me. We

303

played low-stakes poker and chess and talked late into the night, just the two of us. He once told me I had more balls than half the men who flew for him, which was a mixed compliment.' Nic snickered at that.

'Part of the agreement was that he would personally make up a private manifest for each of my flights. No contraband. So, that's how we worked it and everything was fine until my last flight for him. His assistant enjoyed telling me after I landed that my cargo had included illegally mined gold, and she was the one responsible for it being there. She hated my guts.

'But the kicker in all this was that Prospero also had the medallion.'

'Your father and my father sold the medallion to Manoel Prospero?' Nic croaked.

She shrugged and sat back, finally finished with her nursing duties. 'I don't know. I didn't ask how he got it. I just saw it in a case when I went to his office to talk about my terms for flying for him. I pretended I liked it and made him an offer for it. He agreed to that, too, and added on a month's worth of flights to pay for it. Seven months total. He said the medallion made him nervous, like it was cursed or something, and he didn't want to tempt fate any longer. That last flight, the dirty one, was the last payment. He made out a bill of sale for the medallion and gave it to me before I took off. He wanted me to stay on.'

She reached for his hand, lacing her fingers with his. 'I went to his office to pick up the medallion and to find out if he knew about the gold in my last cargo. I was prepared to tell him what I thought of him if he had known, but he wasn't there, nobody was. I typed a note and put it where only he would find it, telling him that now *he* owed *me* and why.

'I took the medallion out of the case and left. By that time, I had everything ready to travel in stages to you, so that's what I did. The gold on my last flight probably came from here. That's all I know about this operation,' she ended.

Nic was silent for a minute then mumbled, 'You ought to be glad I'm impaired. I can't make up my mind whether to arrest you for your own good or make love to you, the woman with more balls than half Prospero's fleet pilots.' His head flopped onto her shoulder and he was asleep.

At least she hoped he was simply asleep. Sighing, she maneuvered him into a prone position then lay down beside him. Her plans had jelled. She went over them in her head while listening to his fever-induced moans and mumblings.

Before dawn she would go back to the cove to steal a dugout and as much gas as it would carry. She'd paddle it downstream to their shelter, which she would somehow mark on the river bank before she left. After she picked up Nic, they would take their chances on the swollen river again, using the motor until they ran out of gas. She would have to paddle after that.

She spent most of the remaining hours of the night holding handkerchiefs wet with rain against Nic's burning brow. Once, as she shifted position within their tiny shelter, her foot slipped and her boot struck the buttressed root. A hollow, drumlike sound seemed to reverberate through the tree itself and echo out into the forest.

Nic stirred and struggled to get to his feet. 'A signal!' he said wildly.

It took all her strength to restrain him. 'No, it was me. I accidentally kicked one of the buttresses. What kind of signal?'

The only sounds were the falling rain, a host of insects singing a chorus, and Nic's short, fast breaths between delirious mutterings.

Later, in a rational moment, he explained. 'Indian hunters pound against buttressed roots with their feet to signal to each other. It carries for miles.' Then he drifted off again.

The knowledge was useless to her as long as they were so close to the miners, but she mentally filed it away for later. Maybe she could maneuver the dugout close to shore and kick out SOS signals. Maybe someone would come. Maybe Grilo was closer than she thought. Maybe Paul would get to them before Nic died of infection. Maybe . . . maybe . . .

She woke before first light with a new idea clear in her mind. Even a small mining operation like this one had medical supplies and a radio. Nic had told her that the shack was a guard post to watch the river approach. If she could just get inside it before she stole the dugout . . .

Nic was resting more quietly, his face drawn and haggard. She kissed him quickly on the cheek and left before she lost the little courage she had gathered.

She used his pocket-knife to cut tiny marks low on the trees, unnoticeable to anyone except herself, as she moved upstream. When she caught sight of the shack, she dropped to her hands and knees and crawled to the boulder they had sheltered behind yesterday. She studied the shack.

It was the only building in the clearing. There were squares cut out of the two side walls and the back wall for windows but no glass was in them. The door faced upstream, the way they had first approached it. Soft dawn light showed beneath the shack because it squatted above the forest floor on short, round stilts, thick cuts of tree trunks by the look of them. Leaf and plant debris had been scraped away from beneath the shack and as far as the beach, leaving a cleared circle of black dirt all the way around the area.

Whispering a prayer, she ran in a crouch to the back of the shack. Immediately her nostrils were assailed by the smell of stale urine coming from the area of the left rear corner. She inched toward the right corner.

Over the thudding of her heart and the rushing water in the sluice, she could hear someone moving around inside. She fell on her knees after they threatened to give way from fear, while a heavy weight rested on her chest. She realized what her fate would be if she was caught, and Nic's as a consequence.

She heard the door open. Peering under the shack, she saw sturdy legs ending in unlaced boots walk around the left side of the building.

She rose to a crouch and crept around the right corner, taking what cover was offered behind the tree trunk stilt. She was ready to take to her heels at the slightest provocation. Glancing quickly behind her, she saw that the beach area was deserted. Felippe relieved himself against a tree. When he turned away, he walked past the shack and took the path that led into the forest.

She retreated to the rear wall of the shack to watch him. As soon as he was out of sight, she put her hands over the raw edge of the window opening and pulled herself up to peek inside. The shack was empty.

Scanning the area once more, she tore around to the front of the shack and leaped up the two wooden steps onto the tiny porch. As she ducked inside and shut the door, she caught a glimpse of a huge dinner bell and rope fastened to the outside wall beside the door. A simple alarm system that would summon armed guards, no doubt.

She could smell the occupant even though he was no longer there. Wrinkling her nose in disgust, she took a quick visual inventory of the room. The walls were bare, except for one lizard and a crucifix. A cot was shoved against one wall. A bottle of liquor sat on the floor near it. A chair sat beside each window. A gun lay on each chair. There was no radio and no food. But sitting in a corner was a dirty white box with a red cross on it and a neat stack of girlie magazines on its top.

Muttering another prayer, she ran to the box, carefully put the magazines on the floor, and opened it. Inside was a big bottle of iodine, cotton balls, a handful of sample packets of antibiotic capsules, rolls of gauze, gauze pads, adhesive tape, and small adhesive strips. She didn't pick or choose, she simply shoved everything into her pockets. With a slapping sound, she replaced the magazines in their place of honor after she closed the lid.

Then she heard it. Whistling.

She dropped to the dirty floor and raised herself just enough to peep out the left side window, the forest side. A different man, fat, black-bearded, and heavy-fisted, with fingers like sausages, was headed for the shack at a fast walk.

She tried to think clearly in spite of the mind-numbing fear that washed over her in a sickening wave. The door was in his full view. If she went out the right side or rear window, he would see her feet and legs in the space beneath the building. If she shot him, others would come. Maybe she could just hit him on the head with one of the guns.

As she picked up the gun on the chair beside her, her eyes fell on the bare, dirty mattress on the cot. Her stomach rolled as a vivid image flashed into her head of those hands and those fingers, instead of Nic's, touching her. She decided to shoot him, if she had to, and take her chances.

She was crawling toward the door, to station herself behind it, when she heard a shout from the forest. Someone was calling the guard back. She scampered back to the left side window in a low crawl. With disbelief she watched the guard walk back the way he had come, muttering.

Thoroughly unnerved, she put the gun on the chair and dove for the right side window, the beach side. As she slid over the edge of the rough-cut opening, her shirt rode up and she scraped her left side painfully on the wood.

She paused long enough at the corner to study the forest path then ran to the boulder. Once she was safely behind it, she started shaking. Her side burned and she felt a warm wetness when she put a hand over the area. It was a very dangerous idea to steal a dugout now. She had spent too much time getting the medical supplies.

But she had no choice. They couldn't afford to waste another day. It would cost Nic too much. So, when she thought her legs would work properly, she rose to her knees to survey the area. Her heart lurched in disappointment as she watched four men, the fat guard among them, walk off the forest path and head directly toward the beach.

It was full light now and she could see that the portable dock had been pushed out into the protected water of the cove and secured to trees on both sides. She scarcely had time to wonder why before she heard the sound of a low-flying plane approaching from upriver.

With a satisfied smile, she settled down to watch it land. Maybe, just maybe, she and Nic could fly down the Sonhos after all.

14

The plane was a moderate-size, two-engine cargo amphibian. It was loaded and rode low in the water. She recognized it immediately because she had flown it several times. It was one of many in Manoel Prospero's fleet of aircraft.

Still, she couldn't believe her eyes when a short, stocky, white-haired figure, with gold flashing at his throat and on his fingers and wrists, stiffly climbed out after the plane taxied up to the dock. The Man himself, Manoel Prospero.

Marcos, his chief pilot, a nice enough guy in a slick kind of way, tied down the plane while Prospero moved off toward the shack. He waved and shouted greetings to someone. Then Gabby noticed the stream of armed men hurrying toward him from the forest, and she sank lower behind the rock.

Prospero, now blocked from her sight by the shack, was apparently on the porch. The alarm bell clanged. She recognized his laugh then his voice inviting everyone to a party that night.

She was torn between getting back to Nic and staying there to learn more. Staying there won. Maybe she would hear or see something that would make her new plan safer for her and Nic.

A long line of miners, skinny men and young boys in tattered clothes, followed the guards. They unloaded boxes of food and supplies and carried them to the hidden mine in an endless loop of moving bodies. Among the boxes she noticed several cases of liquor and overheard shouts about the celebration after the day's work.

Then came the interesting part. After the cargo was off-loaded, Marcos refueled the plane from the fuel drums on the beach. The miners rolled them out, one after another, onto the dock.

They loaded the empties into the plane and moved the remaining full ones on the beach closer to the dock.

'That's it, Marcos. Give me enough to get us to Grilo,' she quietly urged. 'You and the boss just stay put today and party tonight so we can borrow your ride.'

She jogged all the way back to their shelter, following her marks on the trees at a nice trot. The whole forest was wide awake when she got there. So was Nic.

'I thought you had gone on alone,' his hoarse voice said from the shady interior.

She lifted a few of the palm fronds off the roof to let in some light. 'How could you possibly think that, Nic? We're getting out of here tonight, one way or another.'

Before he could question her, she dug into her pockets. There was no way she could hide her medical-supply booty from him, so she simply laid everything out before his disbelieving,

317

outraged glare and waited for the explosion.

It came. His eyes glinted and he spewed a litany of curses in Portuguese, including the word she had used the other day. Finally, in English, 'You went back there? You went back where that Felippe guy could get his hands on you?'

'Yes, I did. And as you can see, I'm back safe and sound. I didn't even have to shoot anybody,' she concluded brightly.

His eyes moved over her, stopped, then widened. Before she realized he had moved, he was on his knees in front of her. One-handed, he yanked her shorts and underwear down over her hip then her shirt up on her left side.

'What the hell is this?' he demanded, his voice rising on the words while he stared at her bloody side.

She tried to reassure him while pulling her clothing back into place. 'Just a scrape, Nic. I promise. Let me do your shoulder then you can help me with my side. You'll see then. Just a scrape.'

He fell back against the root with a groan and covered his eyes with that deft right hand that had nearly undressed her in two moves. 'You'd better tell me all of it. It can't be worse than what I'm imagining.'

She broke open a packet of antibiotics and he took them with a leaf cup of rainwater. She told him her story, in detail, up to the point just before the plane landed, while she cleaned his shoulder with iodine. She managed to eat several bananas at the same time. She covered the wound with gauze and held it in place with the adhesive tape. She left off the sling for now. When she finished all these tasks, she sat back against the opposite root and looked at him.

He sounded defeated. 'I was wrong. It *is* worse than I imagined. And you did it for me.'

She reasoned with him in a soft voice. 'You would have done the same thing for me, only you could never have gotten those shoulders through that narrow window opening.' When he looked up and gave a tiny smile, she continued.

'Besides, I got you into this.' Briefly, her mind wandered back to her time in the shack. 'Man, I really hated to leave that gun,' she said wistfully. 'But he would have known someone had been there if I had taken it.' Nic's quick intake of breath brought her attention back to him.

'Come here,' he said quietly, his eyes glittering.

'Why?' she asked warily. There was an emotion in those beautiful bloodshot eyes and it wasn't passion.

'So I can box your ears,' he growled. 'Or kiss you. I'm a man at war with himself because I want to do both equally at this moment.'

'Then I'll stay right here until the moment passes or until the kiss wins,' she answered, grinning.

He ran his right hand through his

unkempt hair. 'I suppose I was delirious or hallucinating or something, but I thought I heard a plane. And the mother of all bellbirds.'

'You weren't dreaming. I didn't finish my story. Manoel Prospero arrived from upriver in a big, fat amphib full of supplies, including liquor. He rang the alarm bell outside the shack to announce a party tonight. That plane is our ride to Grilo, Nic. We're going to steal it after dark, while everybody is partying.'

'Heaven help us,' was all he said then closed his eyes and kept them closed. 'I'm fading fast, Gabrielle O'Hara. If you need my help with anything, it had better be soon.'

Her side really burned now and she had been trying hard to ignore it. Gingerly, she untied the knot in her shirttails, folded the material up under, and retied it higher under her breasts. She put the iodine and cotton balls where she could reach them then pushed her shorts and underwear down to her hip bone. They slipped down so easily because she had lost weight.

'Nic,' she said softly. His eyes flicked open. 'Can you just clean out my scrape and see if there are any splinters in there? I'll hand you the cotton balls.'

He stirred, nodding his head. 'How — ?' he began, gesturing awkwardly.

She saw the problem and the solution. 'If I lay across your lap, you should be able to manage.'

She carefully draped herself across him and propped herself up on her right elbow. Dousing two cotton balls with iodine, she handed them to him.

She sucked in her breath when he began cleaning away the blood from the outside edges of the scrape toward the center. 'Take it easy, Nic! You're not polishing your shoes, you know,' she informed him.

'Sorry.' He proceeded more gently. 'It's just a scrape, a long, wide one. It looks clean to me.'

He asked for more cotton balls then

helped her cover the seeping area with a gauze pad held on with adhesive strips. When he finished, he eased her shorts into place then patted her on the butt.

She looked at him and felt a tingle of fear. He had a short, bristly beard now, black as the rain forest night. With his dirty, tattered clothing and coloring, he could easily pass for one of the men from the mine, or maybe the medallion's conquistador, except for his eye color. His gray-blue eyes, in sharp contrast between dark hair above and dark beard below, looked right into her soul.

'Boo!' he said then grinned when she jumped. 'What?' he asked.

'You-You're looking very Brazilian right now. Dangerous,' she added in a shaky voice.

His gaze grew more intense and he leaned an inch closer. 'I am dangerous. I'm just too sick to demonstrate how dangerous.'

The scary moment passed when he raised her hand to his lips and kissed her softly on the inside of her wrist. She gasped. Then he quickly brought up both knees, squeezing her close against his chest. With his right thumb and forefinger, he seized a corkscrew curl that rested on her cheek, pulled it straight, then watched it spring back into place.

She let her fingers smooth the dark hair that grew on his chest. 'Nic?'

'What, Copper Top?'

'I want you to know something. When I thought I was drowning in the Sonhos and my life flashed before my eyes . . . ' She hesitated. 'It-It was mostly you.'

He swallowed hard. 'Yeah. Mine were mostly you.'

She smiled and he returned it. 'That plane is our last chance, Nic. You can't go on. If-If something happens tonight and we don't make it, if we never get the chance to explore our love, I want to thank you for being my dear friend and for giving me the best and brightest moments of my life.'

'Oh, Gabby,' he said in a choked voice. 'Oh, my darling Gabby.' And then they simply held each other.

The day passed in a blur of heat and heavy rain. It sapped her strength as she looked for food in the immediate area. She found a few more avocado pears and gave Nic several bites with the capsules. She encouraged him to sip water all day long. He slept most of the day.

In late afternoon she woke him and gave him more antibiotics before they made their way slowly to the boulder near the cove. There was no activity around the beach, plane, and shack. She saw Felippe pass in front of one of the windows.

Gabby spent the remaining daylight hours memorizing their route, their 'flight plan,' to the dock and their salvation that was tied to the end of it. She counted and walked off the steps in her mind, picturing the scene in the darkness.

The skies cleared at sunset. She

realized that if the night was clear, they would be silhouetted against the water if they moved out of the plane's shadow. Nic's fever was so high by then that his body heat dried his wet clothes. She feared he was on the threshold of unconsciousness.

The sudden tropical nightfall fell upon them. One moment there was light, the next there was darkness. Wonderful food smells wafted out of the forest. Gabby's stomach growled in response. Then came the sounds she'd been waiting for: shouts and laughter and singing, the sounds of revelry.

There were no lights, noises, or signs of life around the shack. Felippe had left it at last light.

Nic had fallen asleep the moment they reached the boulder. She shook him gently. 'Time to go, Nic.' She almost snatched her hand away from his hot skin.

'Can't see,' he mumbled.

'I'll help you. Hurry.' She got him on his feet and put her arm around his waist then draped his right arm around her shoulder.

He leaned on her heavily and staggered, making it difficult for her to count their steps. It seemed to take forever just to get around the boulder. She was thankful to see the faint outline of the plane against the light of the rising sliver of moon.

Her foot touched wood and she hurried Nic onto the dock where the plane was tied at a right angle. The co-pilot's side faced the shack. The plane's door opened without a sound.

Nic was more alert now, sensing through his fever haze the danger they were facing. He climbed inside by himself. She buckled him in his seat then slid across his lap to get to the emergency kit behind the pilot's seat. She pulled out the flare gun, loading it then jamming it under the waistband of her shorts.

'What are you going to do with that?' Nic asked, apprehension in his hoarse, weak voice.

'It's part of our insurance policy,' she explained as she searched out the proper tool she needed for her work on the beach.

'Can you start the engines when I tell you?' She showed him where the switches were.

Clouds were rolling in across the moon as she climbed over him, leaving the door open behind her. In a low crouch she made her careful way back to the beach.

Feeling her way along the row of fuel drums on the left side of the beach, she stopped at the last one before the gap. She opened the valve on its top then pushed it over as quietly as possible. Fumes arose around her in a cloud as the first glug of aviation fuel shot out onto the sand. She avoided the stream and crossed the gap to the line of drums on the right side of the beach, stopping at the first one where she repeated the procedure. The two streams joined and formed a pool, saturating the sand with high-octane fuel.

She hurried back onto the dock and slid Nic's machete out of its sheath on her belt. One stroke each and the tie-down ropes were severed and the plane floated free. Immediately it began to drift away from the dock, the fast-moving current of the river reaching even into this protected spot.

She stood ready outside the open door beside Nic. 'Now,' she ordered him quietly.

Bless him, she thought to herself, when the engines roared to life, then idled. At almost the same moment a hysterical medley of clanging came from the alarm bell on the shack's porch. Shouts and gunshots rang out.

Gabby knelt on one knee under the shadow of the right wing, which was rotating slowly over the end of the dock. She was catching some of the backwash from the prop on that side, so she held the flare gun in her right hand and steadied it with her left hand under her wrist, just like Nic had taught her a million years ago. When she fired the flare into the fuel-soaked sand, a wall of flames roared up between them and the figures running out of the forest.

She made a running dive for the door of the plane and Nic's waiting arm. He caught her and pulled her inside by the seat of her shorts. She scrambled across him into the pilot's seat as he slammed his door. In the light from the flames she caught a glimpse of the whites of Nic's eyes showing the whole way around the gray-blue irises.

'Time to get the hell out of Dodge, Nic.' She slowly pushed the dual throttles forward as they moved out into the main channel.

Behind them explosions rocked the forest as the flames reached the other barrels.

'Whatever you say, *querida*. Are we normal yet?' he asked then quietly slipped into unconsciousness.

15

The mission hospital at Grilo stood out like a beacon in the dark jungle because that's exactly what Paul Aguerro set up to guide her to him out of the night sky. She homed in on the clean, strong beam shining straight onto the river. She set the big plane down in the roaring rain exactly where it shone. Ignoring the dock, she simply beached the plane.

She had been brief with Dr. Aguerro on the radio, knowing Manoel Prospero would be monitoring the channels for any clue to his stolen plane. She hadn't even looked in the back. God knew what she was carrying. She'd simply sent out a medical emergency message, her estimated time of arrival, and a request for a light, all in a deep, hoarse voice that disguised her own. She turned off the radio after Paul acknowledged.

He didn't seem surprised that it was she and Nic in a different plane. His questions were directed at Nic's injury and her treatment of it, while two Indians carried a stretcher with Nic on it to the hospital building. When he had the facts, he turned her over to one of the nursing sisters and took Nic to surgery.

When the endless hours of waiting ended and Dr. Aguerro appeared, white with weariness, Gabby was sitting in a chair outside the door, wrapped in her fears and a robe she had borrowed from one of the sisters. Her knees were drawn up to her chin. She was clean and she was fed but she would not sleep until she knew the outcome.

Paul didn't make her suffer any longer than it took him to say the words. 'He will live, thanks to you. He will keep his arm, thanks to you. But I fear he will never have the full range of motion in that shoulder. Is that what you wanted to hear?' At last he smiled.

She nodded, feeling tears stream down her face and not caring. 'Thank you, Paul. May I see him?' she whispered, suddenly exhausted.

'I will take you to him only if you promise then to sleep. Your body, your mind, need to shut themselves off for a while. I will give you something.' He waited for her nod.

He helped her to her feet and as they walked she told him about the friendship that had caught fire.

★   ★   ★

When Nic's beautiful eyes opened and fastened on her two nights later in the surgery ward at Grilo mission hospital, her vigil was over. It took all her self-control to keep from throwing herself onto his chest and sobbing like a frightened child.

'Damn it, Gabby,' he croaked at her. 'You promised you'd grow up ugly.'

'I tried, Nic. Welcome back,' she said

raggedly, holding a shaking cup of water with a straw to his lips.

His hand closed over hers and he stared at her a moment before he drank deeply. 'Are you all right?' he asked in a hoarse voice when the cup was half empty.

She nodded. 'Slight malnutrition, exposure, and dehydration, Paul says. I've had many baths, many meals, and lots of clean clothes while you slept.'

She watched his eyes move to the bandages on his left shoulder then follow the tube up to the IV bag dangling above him.

'That's your antibiotic cocktail.'

He did the same with the IV bag on the other side.

'And that's a midnight snack.'

When he flexed the fingers of his left hand, he sucked in his breath.

'Your shoulder is healing fine now that the infection is under control. You'll need physical therapy for it, though. Paul had to operate to clean everything out.' She didn't have enough breath to add anything else at that moment.

Even if Nic had simply been delirious and didn't love her now that he was lucid again, she would be forever grateful that he was still alive and in the same world with her.

'I'll bet he said that you saved my life, didn't he, Copper Top? Because you did. We made it to Grilo then?'

She nodded and he added, 'I had the craziest dream, Gabby.' When she suddenly went still, he stopped and pinned her with a look. 'It *was* a dream. Wasn't it?'

She shifted uneasily and slowly shook her head.

He thought about it then said in disbelief, 'You stole Manoel Prospero's plane?'

'I'm sorry, Nic. It was all I could think of to do.'

His voice was rising. 'You shot a flare into aviation fuel, like someone out of a Schwarzenegger film, while a bunch of Neanderthals with big guns shot at us?'

She grinned at the memory. 'Yeah, that was really cool!' She caught his look and added soberly. 'Except for the Neanderthals with the big guns, of course.'

His tone said he was a man resigned to his fate and his memories. 'You took off and landed on that river full of debris in the dark.'

She shrugged. 'I used the imaginary cross hairs on the windshield and just aimed at the spotlight Paul set up for us.'

He shook his head. 'Our guardian angels deserve to retire after this.' He looked at her and it was as if he reached inside her and squeezed her heart. 'And what happens now?' he asked softly.

She deliberately avoided his eyes and the real meaning of his question. 'Well, I called in for you. I told your superior how you brilliantly settled the dispute between the Nunes and the Amaral and then nearly died in the jungle in the line of duty because he won't give you a plane that will reach far enough into your territory for you to do your job safely. I told him the least he could do was not reveal our names to Prospero. He agreed, then I asked him to redesign your uniform patches.' She laughed when he made a gurgling sound.

'They're sending a military plane for us as soon as Paul says you're officially out of danger. They're also bringing an extra pilot to take Prospero's plane back to Sao Paulo. I think headquarters wants to take a long look at it.'

His eyes burned into her and he suggested something that neither his boss nor Manoel Prospero could possibly, physically do with the plane. 'That isn't what I meant and you know it.'

She tore her eyes away to watch her hands twisting in her lap. 'I know it wasn't, Nic, and I have to say this before we . . . talk about anything else. Can you ever forgive me for this hare-brained scheme that almost got us killed?'

His voice throbbed with an emotion

she couldn't identify. 'There's nothing to forgive, Copper Top, because I wouldn't have missed it for anything. You accomplished everything you set out to do, with the style of an Amazon warrior princess.'

'I didn't set out to try to kill you, in any kind of style,' she wailed miserably.

'No, but in the process you saved me, in more ways than one. You and this trip up the River of Dreams gave me back my life.' He paused. 'And we've found each other again, in ways I never dreamed of. Or was I delirious the whole time out there?'

She sat down on the edge of the bed, taking his hand. 'No, you weren't delirious the *whole* time. I just wasn't sure you still loved me now that you're in your right mind. What if this is as normal as the two of us are ever going to get, Nic?'

'Then our kids will be the envy of all the other kids on our block.' She gasped at his next words. 'I want two years after we're married, Gabby. Two years alone together before we start filling up those windows with little faces. We'll use the time to fix up the house here for a summer place and to establish ourselves in the States. We can form the air service company if you really want to, but I have my teaching credentials in geology, you know.'

'I like that plan better. I think I'm ready to settle down and keep my feet on the ground for a while. I love you, Nic,' she said softly. 'I've loved you since you kissed me when I was fifteen.'

He reached for her then fell back with a grimace as the IV pumps clattered. 'Blast these things! I can't even hold you. I love you, too, Gabby. Together we'll take whatever life offers us next.'

She snuggled down against his chest. 'While we're fixing up the house, don't forget that you invited me to play Jane to your Tarzan in the rain forest. Then there's my own pet project, methods of keeping fever patients warm at night.' She felt his laughter beneath her cheek.

'I'm looking forward to both, Gabrielle O'Hara Hamilton. Now kiss me before I blow out my IVs,' he said raggedly.

As the night-time symphony of the rain forest embraced them, Gabby realized that as long as she was in Nic's arms, her feet would never touch the ground again.

Epilogue

A week later Gabby and Nic, who was still very weak, walked arm-in-arm through the hastily swept garden toward a make-shift altar she'd patched together from pieces of the fallen lattice roof. Paul Aguerro, a Doctor of Divinity as well as a medical doctor, waited for them in the clearing where their old swing used to hang. She had been delighted when he informed her, 'They have not defrocked me. Yet.' Nic's boss was quietly securing a special license, after the fact.

The pilot of the military plane that brought them from Grilo agreed to stop at the house so they could be married there. All of them, including their witness, Luiz, would fly on to Sao Paulo. Luiz had relatives there. Paul would continue on to Rio for weeks of rest and relaxation. She would check

Nic into the hospital Paul had contacted. Their honeymoon would have to wait.

The seasonal rains were upon them in earnest, and they'd waited for hours for this break. Just as Nic slipped his mother's wedding ring on Gabby's finger, a shaft of sunlight broke through the cloud cover, surrounding them with golden light. Everyone looked up.

Gabby inhaled sharply. The light, broken up by the rain-heavy clouds, created a sunburst, rays shooting out in a glorious halo, just like . . .

'It is a blessing, I think,' Paul said.

'Interest paid in full,' Gabby whispered, then turned back to Nic, to hear a moment later the magical words 'husband and wife.'

Pronunciation List

Aguerro	(Ag-where'o)
Amaral	(Ahm-ar-al')
bromeliad	(bro-meel'ee-ad)
caiman	(kay'man)
Deus	(dee'oose)
Grilo	(Gree'loo)
liana	(lee-ahna')
Luiz	(Lou-ees')
Manaus	(Mahn-owse')
Manoel	(Mahn-o-ell')
Nicolao	(Nee'co-lauw)
Nunes	(Noon'ez)
plantain	(plan'tin)
querido (a)	(ker-ee'doh) (ker-ee'dah)
Rio Sonhos	(Ree'o Sohn'yos)
Sao Paulo	(San Pow'low)
tapirs	(tay'peers)